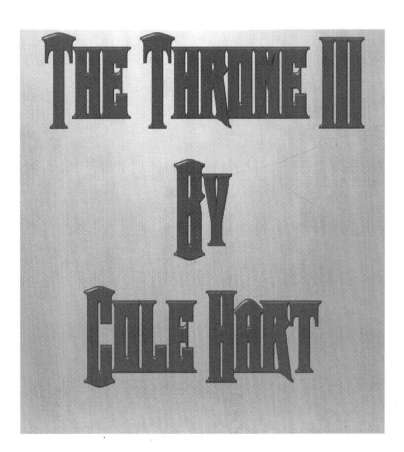

THE THRONE III

BY

COLE HART

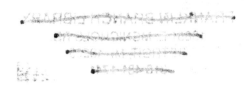

Acknowledgments

From the heart, allow me to thank God first and foremost, because without him, I wouldn't be in this position as a writer, author, and publisher. It's definitely been a long journey for me, and that's good, making me realize that if you really want something out if life you must work for it. Everyday, I'm striving for excellence to better myself and I wanna thank my wife and kids for your ongoing support and my family. You know who you are. Straight up, I salute you all.

Man, big shout out to my home girl, Kiesha, for putting in major werk, and typing up all three parts of The Throne, when it was a bunch of scribble scrabble. To my editor, Tina Nance, I can't thank you enough for preparing all three parts of The Throne for me. To the Bankroll Squad authors and readers, much love and respect to each and every last one of you for showing the love you do. Now this next shout out is special to me, because it belongs to a sixty five year old lady by the name of Mrs. Doretha Jones, and her coworker, Jessica Ramirez, who reads her the books because she's blind. And make sure you let her know we are aware that she has cancer, and that we definitely got her in our prayers.

To my South Carolina homie, Allen Johnson, who orchestrated my live interview with little to nothing to work with. I thank we got the point across, though.

To my brother, David Weaver, I got one question. What they thought we was gonna do? Anyway, I'm focused and ready to take this to the next level. To my home girl, Tiece Mickens, the first author signed with Write House Publishing. Yawl make sure you keep your eyes open for her new summer release, Scarlett. This is Hood Romance at its best. And its coming real soon.

Shout out to my city, Augusta Georgia... and my homies around Georgia. Atlanta... Savannah... MAC- Town, Columbus... Albany and Athens. And the homies from LA to NY. All blue everything party in me once I'm free. As of now, if you incarcerated and you can write and trying to do something, have your people to get at my people and let's C what we can get going.

To my great nephew, Canaan Jordan, make sho you hold your head out there and stay focused. Keep your eyes on the prize and don't get side tracked. You get to Josey. I need a championship ring. Simple as that.

And big shout out to the Haters Circle that thought I wasn't gonna make it. Keep up the good work. You the real reason why I go hard like I do.

PS. To stay on top of Cole Hart and his new releases. Follow him on Twitter @AuthorColehart and like him on FB Author Cole Hart

In Memory

I'm just wondering is it even possible to speak to someone over the phone, a person that you've never met before in person to have such an effect on you that you get a tingling feeling all over your body?

Well, me personally, I did. I actually had a chance to speak with a lady back in December, who didn't appear in the form of an angel, she was an angel. This lady's name is Mrs. Odom. Every time I think about our conversation, I can still remember how she explained to me about the importance of life and how God brings people together for a purpose. For a while, I listened like student in a class room. The knowledge, the wisdom, the understanding. She handed it to me all so quickly, then we laughed together. I asked her questions. She answered them in a soft voice that was turning more into a pulling sound strain. But her words were powerful and strong. And that I can definitely cosign for.

"Baby you're blessed." Came through the phone and spilled over into my soul. Then she added, "You got a wonderful wife and a strong family behind you. And I haven't heard nothing but good things about you."

With her encouraging words, I couldn't do nothing but smile from ear to ear because here was a lady that was born June 21 in the year of nineteen twenty seven. That would put her at eighty five years old. And the way my imagination be running, it seemed that we were having a great conversation face to face over some hot tea in a comfortable living room. Now word for word, I can't remember everything that she said. However, I do remember this. Baby, you gonna be just fine. Just keep God first. That's most important.

We talked for nearly thirty minutes, until she started to get tired on me. And that's when it began to get emotional. No lie, I started feeling some type of way, and I had every reason to. Mainly because here I was having one of the greatest conversations ever with a lady I hadn't ever met before, and even more, she'd only had a few weeks to live. She never spoke about this, but man was this something I had never experienced before. The pain I was feeling was real, like a hand was squeezing my heart. Then we hid our emotions again with laughter and happiness all bundled in one. So while enjoying our conversation, I asked myself how could I forever cherish this moment? And what could I do to pay homage? Outside of our personal promise that she asked of me weeks before she passed away. Then I asked her. How do you spell your name?

She quickly responded: Marion P. Odom. Then she said. You spell my first name like you'd spell a man's name. I made sure I took a mental note of that. I'm still grinning, just remembering her words and how her kindness gave me a relaxed feeling, like another spirit jumped into my body. And I'm sure that everybody that has come in contact with this special and wonderful lady should know the feeling that I'm talking about.

So now for a moment of silence and allow me to share some words with you written from Mrs. Marion P. Odom.

TO THOSE I LOVE

When I am gone, just release me. Let me go, so I can move into my afterglow. You must not tie me down with your tears. Let's be happy that we had so many years. I gave you my love, you can only guess. How much you gave me in happiness. I thank you for the love, you each have shown. But now it's time, I travel alone. So grieve for me a while, if grieve you must. Then let your grief be comforted with trust. It is only for a while that we must part. So bless the memories within your heart. And then when you must come this way alone, I'll greet you with a smile and a Welcome Home.

This book is dedicated in the loving memory of Mrs. Marion P. Odom

June 21, 1927-------January 17,2013

PROLOGUE

Falisa was up bright and early for the special breakfast she had planned for her nurse. She'd been there catering to Falisa, running errands. Going here, going there, not to mention their private group therapy sessions. It had been therapeutic for Falisa to talk about the things she had endured, and for that, she was grateful.

Falisa had the sanitarium's room laid out and lavishly decorated, with sweeping columns and ornamentation, creating the perfect setting for the special event. She buzzed around the room, ensuring that everything was in its proper place. It had to be perfect.

Falisa was fixed up neatly from head to toe. She wore an all-black Yves Saint Laurent women's tuxedo, black shirt and a black tie made of shiny silk. On her feet, she wore a pair of black suede and leather Christian Louboutins. She was healthy as could be, as she moved around the long table that was set up and decorated with expensive dishes just for her and her nurse.

An hour earlier, she'd sent her nurse the exact same Yves Saint Laurent women's tuxedo, along with shoes, tie, and shirt.

When the nurse entered the room, Falisa stopped what she was doing and looked her up and down, examining her facial features. Her hair was let down. It was straight and hanging past her shoulders.

The Throne 3
When she stopped at the threshold, she smiled at Falisa. Turned around slowly, even looking down at herself here and there. "How do I look?" she asked.

Falisa clapped her hands in a slow rhythm. "The question is how do you feel?"

"I feel wonderful. I've never really been into dressing in expensive clothes and Red Bottoms. This is such an honor and a pleasure."

"So you already know how you look." Falisa paused and pushed her jacket open, and placed her hands on her hips. She flashed the nurse the most beautiful smile that she could give, watching her intently. Their eyes locked into each other for at least 15 seconds. Falisa read her entire body language. The nurse's eyes held a glint of desire. Something that Falisa was a master at detecting. "Close your eyes." She told the nurse.

The nurse smiled, nearly like a kid on Christmas. She closed her eyes and Falisa walked toward her. She moved up close to the nurse and stopped directly in front of her. The nurse's eyes were still closed, but she could smell Falisa's closeness. The smile on her lips grew wider.

Falisa leaned in and put her nose on her neck. She sniffed her, and then extended both of her hands, locking her fingers with the nurse's fingers. Her scent was soft and confusing to Falisa's nose. She smelled Chanel… then coconut… maybe Versace.

Falisa pressed her body against the nurse and softly placed her lips on hers. She felt the nurse's entire body relax. Falisa kissed her bottom lip, and then slipped her tongue inside of her mouth. After three seconds, she pulled away from her.

The nurse's eyes finally came open, giving Falisa a seductive stare, mixed with a slight hint of disappointment. Falisa grabbed her by her hand and pulled her to the table that was 10 feet long and two feet wide. Falisa walked her nurse to the other end and pulled her chair out.

The nurse sat down and Falisa pushed in her chair. She watched Falisa sashay back to the other end, thinking to herself, *that is an interesting woman.*

Falisa removed her tuxedo jacket and carefully hung it across the back of her chair, before sitting down. Staring ten feet away into the nurse's eyes, Falisa smiled again. She removed the shiny chrome top and removed her breakfast platter. The nurse did the same thing. Falisa had prepared Belgian waffles, two for each of them, and a small glass of syrup apiece.

Falisa poured syrup over her waffles. "Where did we stop at?" she asked the nurse.

The nurse picked up her small glass of syrup and slowly poured it over her waffles. "You were still in the hospital when Fly killed Zoe, and Amil had been on her worst behavior." She let out a silly giggle.

"Of course, darling. You don't forget anything, do you?" Falisa said while cutting a small square of her waffle with a butter knife, her eyes down on her plate. She shifted them up and looked

The Throne 3
the nurse in her eyes. Falisa felt a tingle all through her body. It was a sad feeling, but a good sad feeling.

The nurse followed suit and cut herself a small square of her own waffle, stuck the fork into it, and carefully eased it inside her mouth. "I just know that dealing with a high caliber woman such as yourself, there's no room for slip ups."

"I like that." Falisa said. "Because slippers always count, and don't ever let anybody tell you differently."

"Slippers always count, I got it," she said cheerfully.

Falisa crossed her legs and took a deep breath. She held her hand up, palms facing out, admiring her huge diamond ring. Her eyes shifted to the nurse. "I'll make it snappy. I'm pressed for time." Falisa said, then added, "But honestly, you're gonna love this."

She leaned forward, and with a small smile, she began to speak.

SBR Publication Presents

Chapter 1

The humming sound that came from the raggedy ventilating system was annoying and adding more problems to Fly's situation. On the third floor of this filthy Fulton County jail, he was balled underneath a mildewed blanket. The room was a small box; four concrete walls, two tube light bulbs built into the ceiling, with a filmy sheet of plastic covering them, which gave off a soft dull glare in his two-man cell.

This particular floor on Rice Street housed the majority of the disabled inmates, like Fly. Some of them were in wheelchairs; others wore shit bags. Most had been in shootouts with the police or had caught the bad end of the stick on a botched armed robbery.

Fly shared his cell with another prisoner, an older black man who was a diabetic and loved to tell the nurse about his sugar level. He had been in prison for the last 23 years for murder and rape. Now he was back in Fulton County jail on an appeal. Fly rarely talked to him because he only spoke about the Georgia prison life. How they did this and how they did that, and he constantly complained about how the county jail food was 10 times worse than their food.

Cole Hart

For the last few weeks, Fly had been back and forth downstairs talking with homicide detectives and attorneys, but the judge wouldn't grant him a bond. That alone took a lot out of him. He'd spoken with Smurf and Papa Bear from the payphones on the wall, trying to explain the situation to the best of his ability about Amil. Papa Bear didn't trust the phones and told him to keep quiet and never discuss his case with any of the prisoners.

Underneath the blanket, Fly scratched his nub and then rubbed it. He thought hard about his situation and the misfortune his own sister had created for him. Fly was angry, and the thought of it was eating him alive. He constantly asked himself, *how do you seek revenge against your own sister? And if you did, what would you do?*

Just then, the door came open from the outside and he felt the cold draft cutting through the mildewed blanket. He opened his eyes, but he didn't remove the cover from his face.

"Breakfast trays just came in, nephew. You eatin'?" He heard the old man ask him.

Fly frowned. He hadn't eaten a good, complete meal since he'd been there. He didn't have an appetite whatsoever. He sucked his teeth, turned over on his side, his back to the door. "I'm a'ight." Fly whispered and tried to find a warm comfortable spot on the thin plastic mattress.

"Nephew, you got to eat something or you—"

"Nigga stop talkin' to me." Fly growled angrily, his voice rose a couple of notches and displayed his aggression.

The old man stood there with his head cocked sideways, his eyes beaming. They were big and decorated with red veins. His hair was thinning at the top. The old man came into the cell, turned his back to Fly, stood over the stainless steel toilet, and urinated.

The smell of his urine was strong, and when it rose through the blanket and up into Fly's nostril, he frowned and growled again. "Damn, flush that stankin' ass piss, nigga."

The old man was already tired of Fly's mouth. He flushed the toilet and shook himself off, then unrolled a few sheets of tissue and wiped off the seat less toilet. He flushed again, went to the small sink and washed his hands. He stood there, then turned around, staring at the knot under the blanket where Fly laid.

"Nigga, you talkin' like you a muthafuckin' gangsta or something." He paused, then added, "I know yo' case, I seen you on the news. You a bitch killa'. And where I'm from, niggas who kill bitches don't get no muthafuckin' respect." Then he stood there, turning his hands into tight fist waiting on Fly to turn over and get up out his bunk.

Fly didn't move. He lay underneath the blanket motionless. "So, if I killed you... Considering you a bitch ass nigga, I guess my respect level will go even lower. I'm a made man, and where I'm from, yo' opinion don't mean shit."

The old man wasn't expecting to hear that. He stood still, never taking his eyes away from Fly. He knew with a statement like that, Fly had to be death struck. However, he was trying to get one murder case off his back, and he definitely didn't want to catch another one. Besides, he felt a bit sorry for the boy. It can't be easy

Cole Hart

to lose a leg at such a young age. He decided to cut him some slack… this time. Without another word, the old man unballed his fist, turned around, and walked back out the cell and into the dormitory.

When Fly heard the door close, he turned over and sat up, snatching the wool blanket from the upper half of his body. He rubbed his nub with both hands. Looking down at his half leg, he cursed himself. "Nigga you handicap, mentally and physically." He closed his eyes. "Amil, you a real bitch."

Out of anger, he balled up his right hand into a tight fist and, *Wham… Wham… Wham.* He slammed it into the open palm of his left hand, staring down at the floor. He turned his head and looked at his prosthetic leg, sitting in the corner at the foot of his bunk. He just couldn't believe that his own sister had that much hatred and betrayal built up inside of her, that she would try to put him away for the rest of his life.

He thought back to when they were children. The love they had between them was unshakable. Amil idolized her big brother, and he loved her just as much. Fly could no longer blame her behavior on her kidnapping ordeal. It had definitely damaged her, but after what she had done to him, he had no choice but to accept the hard truth. Amil had more of Timbo in her than Falisa. And in his eyes, that was bad blood.

He leaned back against the wall and folded his arms across his chest, looking down his nose. "Bitch, you dead." he finally whispered.

The cell door came open and the old man entered with a thick brown plastic tray with five separate slots. There was a clump of unsweetened oatmeal in the main slot, two slices of fake bologna and one hard biscuit. He shoved the tray in Fly's face. "Take dis' shit, nigga, foe yo' ass starve to death."

Fly's eyes traveled from the floor, looking at the old man's crusty toes emerging from a pair of brown open toe shower slides and on up to the tray. His stomach rumbled from hunger. Then he looked up into the old man's eyes. Fly felt his mouth twitching, then another stomach growl. He finally reached for the tray.

The old man put the tray in his hand, turned around, and exited the small cell. He closed the door behind him.

Fly sat the tray down on the foot of his bed, took both of the thin slices of meat and made a small sandwich with the biscuit. He chewed and swallowed so fast, he didn't even taste it.

The old man came back through the door with another plastic tray and a Styrofoam cup filled with steaming coffee. He closed the door with his foot, went over to the metal desk, and sat down with his back to Fly. He sipped his coffee, then looked back at Fly and noticed he'd cleaned the tray.

"Go ahead, nephew. Eat dat shit." The old man said as he handed Fly the tray.

Fly's eyes met his again. He slowly reached for the tray and sat it down on top of the first one, stacking it like a Lego building block. Once again, he took the two pieces of meat, wrapped them

The Throne 3

both around the bread, and brought the pitiful little sandwich to his lips.

As he bit down into it, he cut his eyes at the old man and caught him removing four glazed Krispy Kreme doughnuts from a brown paper towel.

"Krispy Kreme doughnuts came with the breakfast tray?" Fly asked, with a mouth full of food.

"Nawh," The old man said. "Dees folks don't let us eat good like dat'."

"Where you get 'em from, then?"

"Now you all in my business, nephew. Prison rule one. Mind ya' own business." He bit down into one of the doughnuts and chewed slowly, closing his eyes and savoring the flavor, as if he was eating fresh lobster tails imported straight from Maine.

Fly watched him, fascinated by his apparent rapture at having a damn donut. No one in his circle acted that way about food. Without responding, Fly finished off the small biscuit and meat sandwich and turned his attention away from him.

Three minutes passed, and the old man said, "I'ma plug you in wit my connect, nephew."

Fly didn't respond. He flipped the blanket from the lower half of his body and slid down, gripping a metal handrail near the toilet. He propped himself up with his fist and stood at the sink on one leg. He looked at himself in the mirror. His dreads were a mess, and he was growing a thin beard. He pressed the cold button,

Cole Hart

10

cupped one hand underneath the water, and sipped from his hand. Then he hopped to the door on one foot as if he was playing hopscotch. He looked through the small glass and didn't see anything of interest.

He turned and hopped back to his bunk and sat down, turning his eyes directly on the old man. "What connect?"

The old man was stuffing the last bit of his second doughnut in his mouth. "The white nurse downstairs that gives me my insulin shot in the morning."

Suddenly, Fly began to find the old man a lot more interesting. His ears became more in tune. "What about her?"

"See, back at prison, we…"

That's when Fly snapped. His hand shot out like a bolt of lightning. He grabbed the old man under his chin and lifted his head. The old man's eyes widened with fear. "She ready to work, she'll bring me anything I can pay for."

"Pull it off, and I'll get you whatever you want." Fly responded.

"Enough said. Now get yo' muthafuckin hands off me."

Chapter 2

The following morning, Smurf pulled into the parking lot of a public plaza on Cascade road. He parked in front of the GNC health store in a rental van and switched off the engine while waiting on the nurse that worked at Fulton County jail to arrive. Smurf stared through the front glass as cars approached him. His eyes shifted to the rearview mirror when he noticed a sky blue Honda Accord pulling in behind him with a middle-aged white woman behind the wheel.

It was her, and that relieved him because he wasn't comfortable sitting out there like that. She flashed her headlamps and Smurf caught it. He opened his door and stepped down, dressed in steel toe boots and a Dickie uniform. His dreads were pulled back and tucked into a tight ball. Smurf had a cold aura about him, but he never physically displayed anger. When he got to the driver side window, she instantly rolled it down and smiled at Smurf.

Smurf gave her his hand. "Good Morning."

The nurse was a chubby faced red head with a few freckles, thin lips, and a small nose. When she grabbed Smurf's hand, she smiled. "Good Morning," she said.

"I need you to get on the passenger side with me."

"Should I lock my car?" she asked.

"We're not going nowhere. I just want to give you everything real quick."

She switched off the engine, grabbed her handbag from the passenger seat and stepped out. Smurf got in the van and she sashayed around to the passenger side. He pressed the button for the automatic locks and she climbed up and closed the door behind her. Smurf reached in the rear and pulled up a mid-sized nylon duffel bag. He dropped it in her lap, and before he unzipped it, he cut his eyes up at her.

"The first rule. Don't rush and try forcing a piece that won't fit."

Her eyes softened, giving Smurf a sympathetic stare. She touched her chest with her left hand and slowly shook her head. "Oh no, whatever you tell me to do. And besides, I'm not trying to lose my job."

Smurf stared at her for a few more seconds, allowing her words to register in his head. He unzipped the bag as he scanned parking lot. A Fulton County patrol car was approaching. Smurf waited until he passed before removing anything from the bag. After the police car eased over the speed bump and continued on, he removed a rubber-banded bundle of money.

"This is five grand. This is yours, put it up." he handed it to her.

The Throne 3

She grabbed the money. "Damn! I wasn't expecting anything like this." she said happily, and then dropped it into her bag.

The next thing Smurf removed from the duffel bag was a Nokia cell phone and charger, still in the plastic. "You sho' you can get the phone in?" he asked.

"Trust me, I can get it in." she shot back. Pure confidence was in her voice.

When he gave her the phone, she placed it in her bag. Then he came out with two ounces of cocaine and two compressed ounces of exotic marijuana, everything packaged and bundled. "This goes to the old man." He handed that to her. Then he said, "You got my number, call me when they get it. I want you to make sho my nigga get whatever he want. Food... whatever. Okay?"

She stared at Smurf in admiration, and then she said, "Can I ask you a question?"

"What is it?" Smurf asked.

"If I happen to get caught, can I work for you?"

"That shouldn't be a problem."

The old man crept back into the cell at 5:43 a.m., he'd just come back from taking his insulin shot and picking up his package from the nurse. The old man closed the door behind him and

Cole Hart

14

flipped on the light. Fly was in a deep sleep, and dreaming that he was in Paris, having lunch with a celebrity. The old man tapped him on his shoulder, and then he began removing the contents from his drawers and inside his waistband.

He removed the phone first and the charger next. Fly took it and wiped his eyes with his fingers. He squinted against the bright cell light. The old man removed the cocaine and marijuana and stuffed it all inside a hole in his mattress. He went to the door and stood guard while Fly got on the phone.

When Fly turned on the power, the small screen illuminated. He waited for a signal, and then punched in Smurf's number. It rang three times before he heard Smurf's voice on the other end. "Hey, what's up, brah?"

Fly actually broke into a smile for the first time since he'd been incarcerated. "Damn, brah." He finally found the words. "Some kind of way, I got to get up out this shit."

"I spoke with Falisa." Smurf said. "She's out the hospital and she's doin better. Amil, on the other hand, is definitely on some other shit."

"I don't even wanna talk about that bitch, Smurf."

"She still your sistah."

Fly took a deep breath, and changed the subject. "What the lawyer talkin' bout? I need a bond."

"They ain't talkin shit about no bond. Damn, Fly, then it happened the day after your birthday. If you would've been sixteen, we could've taken control of the situation."

"Well, I'm seventeen now, and we still gonna take control."

Fly's eyes went to the back of the old man's head. He saw his hand raise and his fingers snap, giving Fly a signal that the police was making a round. Fly dropped the phone underneath the blanket and the old man turned on his acting skills as if he was talking to Fly.

"I'm tellin' you, nigga, the Falcons going to the super bowl."

Fly looked up at him and smiled. "I agree," was all he said. When his eyes went to the window he saw the face of a Sheriff looking at him, then he went on by. The old man checked the door to see if he'd left. He turned and gave Fly a signal, and Fly picked up the cell phone and resumed his conversation.

"I'm back, brah."

"Do I have to tell you to be careful in there?"

"No, but you do have to tell me how you gon get me out of here."

Smurf took a deep breath on the other end. Silence hung in the air for a second or two.

"Let me find out what the attorneys are talking 'bout. But I know we'll have to wait until your mother gets herself back together. Cause while Amil is in position, ain't nothing happening."

"I need a number on Iris."

"That mean you'll have to speak with Amil. They got it where Iris is Amil's eyes and hands, and she never leaves her side." Smurf said. "Just hold tight for a few days until we come up with something."

"Brah, listen. Go see my mama ya' self and explain to her the situation."

"I will, and I'll do it ASAP again. The first time she refused to listen because she figured you would've handled the situation differently."

"A'ight. Well, next time I will handle it different." Then he hung up in Smurf's face.

Chapter 3

Two more months passed slowly. Fly was nearing the end of his rope. His time at the county had become slightly more bearable; thanks to Karen, the helpful nurse. She kept him well stocked with good food, good weed and even some nice magazines to release some pressure on. Fly was ready to go. Being locked down wasn't for him. He was worried about his mother and he missed the game.

On this particular morning, a team of police was escorting Fly to the Fulton County courthouse. They pushed him in his wheelchair and had him wearing a bulletproof vest and armor-piercing helmet.

"Murderer! Animal! Sick ass bastard!" Fly heard onlookers shout as he was wheeled into the courthouse. Others just watched and pointed at him as if he was some type of mad suicide bomber or serial killer.

There were Fox 5 news reporters taking pictures and other T.V. News trucks everywhere. Fly kept his head down to avoid cameras; he knew what he'd done was brutal and unnecessary, but he couldn't care less at that point. He was fighting for his life. The prosecutors wanted to nail him to the cross and send him to Jackson State Prison.

Inside the courtroom, there were people everywhere, crammed together on the benches. His defense team was there also; two well-dressed and groomed white guys who had a lot of influence throughout the city of Atlanta. There were also two women; one blond, with long legs and glasses and another Korean female who popped gum uncontrollably. On the first set of benches behind the defense table, Fly noticed Iris and Amil sitting next to each other. Then he noticed Smurf and January sitting on the second row. The officer parked Fly next to the team of attorneys and removed the helmet from his head. His dreads were pulled back into a neat ponytail at the nape of his neck. Fly spun around, making eye contact with Amil.

She looked at him for no longer then three seconds and then she focused her attention on something else.

The judge entered and immediately the burley bailiff shouted, "All rise."

Everybody in the courtroom rose to their feet, except for Fly. He scanned the courtroom; something wasn't right. He could feel it running through his veins. Through the many faces that filled the courtroom, Fly noticed a female staring at him suspiciously.

"You may be seated." The judge said.

Fly turned his wheelchair to an angle. He looked around again and made out a face on the side of the courtroom. A man with thick bifocal glasses and a salt –n-pepper afro stared back at him.

Fly wasn't tripping, he knew. But behind it all, he knew that the man disguised in the wig and glasses was none other than his brother, Hawk. He felt panicky. He looked back toward the other side for the girl that had been watching him. She pretended to be looking somewhere else. The judge was saying something, but Fly wasn't paying attention. He spun around and looked at Iris.

"That nigga Hawk is here. Get Amil out of here."

Immediately, Iris stood up.

Then, from out of nowhere, a cloud of smoke appeared and people begin jumping up from their seats, screaming and yelling. Another smoke bomb was released and Hawk appeared directly in front of Fly with a Heckler & Koch .40 caliber gripped inside a gloved hand. When the shot went off, the courtroom exploded into pandemonium.

Fly flipped from his wheelchair. He saw Amil standing over him in tears.

Hawk aimed his gun at Amil and squeezed the trigger. The bullet pierced her chest and she dropped to the floor next to Fly.

"Killed you and your sister, you bitch ass nigga."

When Fly rolled from his bunk, he hit the floor and stared around the two-man cell in confusion. His breathing was heavy and his chest was rising and falling. He looked up and saw the old man looking down at him.

"Demons chasing you again." he said to Fly. Then he stood up and helped Fly from the floor.

Fly got up. Small beads of sweat appeared on his forehead. He sat on the bed and thought about the dream that he'd just had. His dreads hung loose and wild. When his eyes finally settled on the old man, he saw him sniffing cocaine from the back of his knuckle. For a brief moment, his mind flashed back to the high he used to get from the Oxycontin pills. He dismissed the thought as quickly as it came. It wasn't important.

Fly felt that something wasn't right and he trusted his gut feelings. He took his prosthesis from the corner and strapped it on. Then he reached for his phone.

Chapter 4

Down in Miami, Florida, the all-white mansion that Falisa owned was crawling with a team of nurses and doctors that made sure Falisa was healing correctly. Tonight, she was laying in her huge king sized bed, sipping freshly squeezed orange juice from a straw.

Amil stood next to her, brushing her mother's hair while they talked. When the phone rang, Amil stopped and answered it. "Hello."

"Let me speak to Mama." Fly said in a demanding tone.

"I'm sorry, but you have the wrong number."

"Bitch, put my goddamn mama on the phone. Now!" Fly roared angrily and loud enough that Falisa heard him.

Amil eyes squinted, she thought about just clicking him off the line, but instead she handed her mother the phone.

Falisa took the phone and pressed the speaker button. "Hey."

"Listen, Ma, I believe the nigga Hawk is here in Georgia. I need to get out."

"Your trial date is in a couple months, Fly, and…"

"No… I need to be out. Did you not hear me? I said these niggas is here."

"How do you know they're there?" Amil asked. She rolled her eyes as if to tell her mother that he was lying. Then she asked, "Have you seen him?"

"I'm not talking to you, Amil. Stay out my fuckin' business."

Falisa looked up at Amil and placed her finger on her lips. Amil took a deep, disgusted breath, turned around and exited the room. She didn't have to be there to hear the conversation. She'd had everything bugged.

When the door closed, Falisa took the phone off speaker. "Go ahead." she said.

Fly got quiet for a moment, and then his voice came through the phone. "I had a dream, they here, Mama. I'm telling you."

"Well, I'll call Papa and Pig Man."

"I need to be there." Fly screamed through the phone at her.

"You better tone your voice down, Fly. This is not Amil." She responded calmly.

Silence hung in the air between the two of them. Then Falisa said, "You had the best position, the best opportunity that any young man could want in this line of work."

"I understand that, but even you said yourself that nobody is perfect and you must learn from mistakes."

"And have you learned, Fly?"

Another short silence.

"Yes, Mama, I've learned."

"Now, if you and Amil would call a truce on your little conflict, we can go ahead and start the process."

"Put her on the phone."

Falisa took the phone away from her face as a sharp pain raced through her body. She cringed a little, but quickly caught herself. Her ribs weren't completely healed yet.

"Amil." she called out softly.

Nearly an entire minute went by and Amil didn't answer. Falisa's eyebrows bunched together out of curiosity. Then when she got ready to call her again, the door came open

Amil peeped her head inside. "Yes mother?" She sounded calm and polite.

Falisa cranked her finger and Amil walked inside and closed the door. She stood beside the bed as Falisa held the phone pressed against her chest. "Y'all make your peace with one another. Right now." She handed Amil the phone.

Amil walked over toward the window while talking. "Hello, Fly. Allow me to apologize to you for my actions."

"Apology accepted." He sighed, and then added, "I'm sorry for my actions as well. Okay?"

Amil smiled, and then she turned and faced Falisa who was already watching her. "Only way we'll be able to get you out is…"

"Hey." Falisa shouted and interrupted her. Falisa placed her finger on her lips. Then she reached for the phone.

Amil handed it to her.

"Be patient." she said into the receiver.

"Alright," Fly whispered. "I love you."

"Love you too, baby." She ended the call. Then she looked at Amil. "Let's prepare."

Amil nodded and swallowed her pride on the strength of her mother. But deep down inside, she did not intend to release her seat on The Throne.

Chapter 5

Hawk was indeed in Atlanta, and he had an exclusive penthouse apartment in mid-town. The penthouse was decorated with Italian furniture and a two hundred gallon fish aquarium built into the wall of the front room. Hawk sat in the comfortable chair that was positioned nearly six feet away from the aquarium, smoking a rolled blunt of exotic marijuana and staring at the four-foot long Hammerhead shark that swam back and forth. The walls that surrounded Hawk were decorated with beautiful paintings by Andy Warhol. There was a painting of the Mona Lisa, but it wasn't authentic. However, the art gave the penthouse a classical taste and that classical taste gave Hawk a sense of power. He was definitely on top of his game, worth a few million dollars, and had himself a team of goons up and down the east coast.

Today, he was surrounded by a close-knit team. His older comrade was named Rolex. The close circle called him Lex, for short. He went into retirement years ago, right after they'd kidnapped Amil. But all the retaliation from The Georgia Boys, as they called them, was enough to bring him out of retirement to ride with his comrade, Hawk.

Across the room, a dark skinned female with an oval shaped face and a long scar running from her earlobe to the corner of her lip was stretched across a leather couch. She went by the name, Boo. She was a rough chick from the Bronx who grew up in Baltimore. Hawk found her through a few of his sources, and her name held some weight because she'd beat a couple of murders.

Hawk's plan was to come down and stick around Georgia for a little while, and maybe he'd get lucky and bump into Fly. Then, a couple of months ago, he saw his enemy's name and face on the news and in every Atlanta Journal Constitution that had been released since then. Hawk was on top of the case for sure; he'd even mapped out his blueprint for what he was going to do. It was simple. Catch his sister and mother when they leave the trial, because he was sure that the courts would find him guilty. Hell, he threw a woman over thirty stories to her death, in broad daylight. Murder was definitely the case. So now, he would wait until everything unfolded. This was a mandatory and personal decision. They kidnapped his friend, Ox, and he in turn, sacrificed himself.

Hawk relaxed in his recliner. He set the blunt in the glass ashtray that sat inside the arm of the huge chair. He finally closed his eyes, his fingers steepled together. In his comfortable mind state, he was enclosed inside a beautiful green garden with pigeons walking around on a smooth slab of concrete. A waterfall was to the left of him along with an attractively landscaped lake that seemed to stretch over 100 acres.

That vision faded, and he thought about how they gunned down Cory, and how they killed his mother. *Retaliation is a must,* he thought to himself. He took a deep breath and sat up in his chair. He was beginning to get a headache.

Smurf stood in front of his dresser mirror, staring at his reflection. His girl, January, was standing behind him, her arm across his shoulder and hand pressed against his linen shirt. When he turned and faced her, his hands slipped around her waist and their lips met.

"Where you going?" she whispered to him between kisses.

"I got to fly down to Miami to see Falisa."

"I'd love to go with you."

"It's personal business, baby. I'll be back in a couple days." he kissed her forehead.

Smurf rubbed his hands down to the small of her back, then out of the blue, he fell down to one knee and produced a five-carat diamond and platinum ring. When he looked up into January's eyes, she was already near tears. Her hands covered her mouth and she tried her hardest to keep from crying.

"Will you marry me, baby?" Smurf asked.

January stood there, tears pushing out of her eyes, to the point that she was choking. She fanned herself with her hands, then dropped to her knees and faced Smurf. They smiled and kissed again. Smurf took her hand and eased the ring on her finger. She looked at it, her heart pounding erratically. Then she wrapped her arms around his neck, her forehead pressed against his and their eyes penetrating each other.

Smurf kissed January again. His love for her consumed his heart. This was a new chapter in his life and he was excited for their future.

He finally stood up and she did too. "Let me get out of here." he told her.

She held onto him, her tiny hands wrapped around his wrist just before he could turn around, when he looked in her eyes she displayed pure loyalty. Then she smiled. "I love your ass to death." She stood on her toes and kissed his lips again.

Outside, in his four-car garage, Smurf pressed a remote automatic car starter on a low-key Ford Taurus. He got inside and closed the door. He pressed another button for the garage door to open. He looked into his rearview mirror and carefully backed out of the garage and picked up his cell phone. He punched in a single digit number and recognized Papa Bear's voice instantly.

"In route?" he asked from the other end.

"In route." Smurf responded. He pressed another button and ended the call.

He was on his way to Augusta.

Chapter 6

During Smurf's trip to Augusta, he thought about his life and everything he'd been through since he'd met Fly. Fly was definitely like his little brother, and he loved him just as he would if they'd come from the same womb. Riding down I-20 and about thirty minutes away from his exit, he was tailing an eighteen-wheeler when his phone rang.

"How you doing?" A soft elegant voice asked from the other end.

Smurf paused briefly, making sure the voice was registering. Then Amil's photo popped into his vision.

"Smurf?" she said. It came as a question this time.

"Hey, what's up, Amil?"

"Just wanted to call you... I really wanna apologize to you for my actions and things like that. And also wanna know if you'll accept my apology?"

Smurf rode in silence, pondering her words and occasionally checking his rearview mirror. Amil was sounding like a grown up, honest and sincere. He finally cracked a smile. "I accept your apology, Amil."

"Phew… I was holding my breath," she said with a nervous laugh. "When you get to Papa, I'll call you back." Then the line clicked off.

Smurf looked at the phone briefly, and then he tossed it in the passenger seat. The trip from Atlanta to Augusta only took an hour and a half, and thirty minutes later, he was on Papa Bear's property, creeping through the uneven dirt road while some Garth Brooks song happened to be playing on his radio. He frowned and asked himself, *how the hell my radio station change by itself?* He turned it off and finally came to the opening of Papa Bear's farm.

There was another Ford Taurus, identical to the one he was driving, parked in front. Pig Man stepped out from the driver's side just as he was parking. Smurf looked at him through the glass, and noticed that the burned part of his face had been repaired. The trunk was already open.

Smurf grabbed his bag, slung it over his shoulder and closed the trunk. Then he and Pig Man begin walking toward each other. They embraced, clapped each other on the back, and separated. Pig Man removed a pack of Newports and thumped one from the pack. He was definitely a nicotine fiend.

"What's in the bag?" Pig Man asked Smurf while lighting his cigarette.

Smurf looked up at him. "Just a change of clothes. A fatigue suit and a vest."

"Always business," Pig Man said. He exhaled a cloud of smoke from his mouth. His eyes squinted and he asked in a lower tone of voice. "Is it true that Amil got Fly fucked up wit' dat' murder?"

Smurf stood quiet for a brief moment. He heard footsteps and a loud chain rattling. He turned around and saw the pit-bull, Bo, coming from around the side of the house with ripping muscles as he angrily pulled a huge tractor tire attached to a thick chain.

Smurf looked back at Pig Man. "Somethin' like that." He knelt down in front of Bo and rubbed the top of his head. "Hey boy." Smurf said to the dog.

Then Papa came from the rear of the house, dressed in his usual attire— a Dickie suit. He saw Smurf and they embraced. "Yawl come on inside."

Smurf and Pig Man followed him around the side of the house and they all went through the back door. They took a seat at the kitchen table. There was a bowl of apples and oranges in the center of the table, along with a cordless phone. He punched in a number and Amil's voice came from the other end.

"Hello Papa," she said.

Papa Bear pressed a button and turned the phone on speaker so everyone in the house could hear her.

"How you doin', sweetheart?"

Then Pig Man spoke. "Hey, baby girl. You alright?"

SBR Publication Presents

"I'm fine, Pig. And you?"

"Couldn't be better."

"That's good," she said. Then she asked. "Are you there, Smurf?"

Smurf had his elbows on the table and his hands propped under his chin. "I'm here."

"Good. I'm glad everyone could come out on behalf of my mother. We're good on these lines, meaning we can speak freely. These phones can't be bugged, tapped or traced. So with that said, we're open for any suggestions that anybody may have for getting Fly out."

Everybody was quiet. Nothing was said as everyone wrestled with their individual thoughts.

Smurf looked at Papa Bear, Pig Man looked at Smurf, and Papa Bear slowly shrugged his shoulders and shook his head from side to side.

Amil's voice broke the silence. "Everybody, Iris just came in."

"Hey Iris." Smurf said.

"Hello lady." Pig Man said.

"Iris." Papa Bear whispered, and then he rubbed his hand across his face. He seemed to be lost in deep thought.

33   Cole Hart

"Hello everyone," Iris greeted them all at once. "Who can we pay up there to release him by accident?" she said, cutting right to the chase.

"That was the first suggestion that came to mind." Papa Bear said. "But since the Fulton County system is already under investigation, a lot of people are hesitant to move in our favor."

"We got to be able to rub shoulders with some politicians in Atlanta." Pig Man said. Then he went on. "We need Falisa to pull some strings or something."

"Everybody got to know that we're in position to pull major moves. We're connected, but not with the state." Amil said.

"Let's wait until he goes to court and then break him out." Smurf said. "We got enough niggas on our team to pull it off."

"And what if it doesn't go as planned?" Iris responded.

Silence hung in the air again.

Then out of the blue, Amil said calmly, "I think I got it."

Papa Bear slowly shook his head. Smurf sat back in his chair and folded his arms across his chest. Pig Man snuffed his cigarette butt in the ashtray.

They all knew that if Amil had a plan, they had to work.

Chapter 7

When Falisa called Dr. Aston Oliver to come to Miami, he was there within 24 hours. Amil was there to greet him upon his arrival at the all-white mansion. She greeted him with a firm handshake and introduced herself. He was alone, dressed in a beige wrinkled linen suit and leather sandals.

"I'm Dr. Oliver," he said with a bright smile. His teeth were Colgate commercial ready.

Amil sidestepped and allowed Aston to come in. He stopped in the foyer, awaiting her direction. Although this was not his first visit to the mansion and he knew his way around pretty well, his impeccable manners dictated that he wait for his host.

Amil closed the door and led the doctor into the living room. She was dressed in a cream-colored blouse, jeans, and low heels. Her toes were exposed and neatly pedicured. A soft jasmine scent trailed behind her. Amil, at fifteen years old, was blossoming in to a beautiful young woman. She was very feminine and aware of her body. This made her more treacherous, because she had definitely had a dangerous side to her that she was mastering the art of disguising, more every day. Now she was armed with the ultimate distraction—her feminine wiles.

The Throne 3

Amil offered Aston a seat on the leather love seat. "What would you like to drink?" she asked him. Her eyes focused directly on him, as if the fate of the world depended on his answer.

"Vodka." Aston replied in his thick Brazilian accent.

"Fruit…. cheesecake?" she shrugged with a smile.

He cleared his throat. "Just vodka."

Amil nodded and walked off. She rounded the corner and stepped into the open kitchen. Papa Bear was standing next to the center island holding a leather briefcase. His eyes were on Amil.

"Go ahead and get his drink. I'll take the money out to him." With that said, he walked off with the briefcase clutched in his right hand.

When he got to the living room, Papa Bear stopped directly in front of Aston and politely sat the briefcase on the mahogany table in front of him. He carefully placed it bottom down and unsnapped the gold plated buttons. He flipped the top open, revealing rows of crisp one hundred dollar bills.

Papa Bear looked at Aston. "Seven hundred and fifty now." he said. "After the surgery, you'll get one million wired directly into your account." Papa Bear extended his hand out to Aston and he shook it.

Papa Bear walked off as Amil was returning with the double shot of vodka for. Carrying it carefully in her hand, she sashayed over to Aston and placed the glass in his hand. She looked at the money, closed the briefcase, sat in the chair across from him and crossed her legs.

Her eyes bored into him. "Of course, you know I'm only the voice for my mother."

He turned back his drink. When the warm liquor hit his throat and stomach, he made a "Hah" sound and sat the glass down. He finally nodded his head.

Amil uncrossed her legs and sat on the edge of the chair, placing an elbow on each of her knees, and her hands underneath her chin. "We have a man whose status is unknown to us. And what we would like you to do is change his face."

"That's not a problem, that's my profession," he said cheerfully. He had actually expected them to request a miracle.

"But we need you to make him look exactly like my brother. And his prints must be removed."

Aston paused. His eyes didn't blink. A deep sigh escaped his lips. "I can't make any promises on that." he said shook his head.

Amil noticed a hint of rejection in his voice. "Papa," she called out.

Papa Bear appeared at the edge of the living room. She looked up at him and held up one finger. "Bring me one more briefcase."

Without a word, Papa Bear spun around and faded away. Amil sat back in her chair. She was patient. She crossed her legs again and looked the doctor square in the eyes with a beautiful smile. No more than a minute went by and Papa Bear was back with another briefcase. He carefully set it on the table, on top of the first briefcase. He clicked the gold plated locks and opened it.

Still, Papa Bear hadn't said a word to Aston. He made eye contact with him and the look that Aston caught was cold and deadly. Papa Bear quickly turned his face into a smile, and then he walked away.

Aston's eyes went back to Amil, down to the money and back up again. He rubbed his hands together and cleared his throat. "Let's put everything on the table. What all do you need me to do?"

Amil sat up in her chair, striking a Malcolm X pose with her finger resting against the side of her face. "This is more like an emergency. We have the guy here. We have all the equipment here that you'll need, and I'm interested in being your assistant if it's not too much to ask."

Aston listened carefully to Amil's words. He sat back and replayed everything she'd just said in his head. "So, you have everything I need and you wanna be my assistant?"

She gave him a smile, and then in a soft polite voice, she said, "Yes sir."

"So where is the unknown person?"

Amil stood up. She motioned for him to stand up as well.

Aston stood up, and Papa Bear appeared. The three of them walked through the mansion, with Papa Bear in the lead. They walked directly behind him, bypassing wooden doors on either side of the corridor. Papa Bear stopped in front of a thick wooden door on the left. He turned the knob and pushed it open. When he stepped inside, Amil and Dr. Aston came in behind him. The room had been turned from a custom bedroom into a nice sized operating room that was equipped with everything the doctor needed.

Aston entered the room and headed straight to the surgery lights. To his left was an expensive anesthesia machine. Aston slowly walked around it, silently evaluating. His hard bottom sandals clicked against the tile as he moved. He checked his infusion pumps. There were several scalpels neatly lined up next to each other on a black velvet cloth. The silicone was next to them.

Aston loosened his tie. "This is an excellent operating room," he said to no one in particular. His hands went to his waist, and then he turned around and faced Amil and Papa Bear. "So where's our guy?"

Papa Bear walked toward the back of the room, to another thick wooden door. He turned the knob and walked inside. The small room was an upgraded walk-in closet, the size of a prison cell. Ox was sitting in the corner, his knees pulled up into his stomach and his hands were cuffed in front of him. Ox looked tired and drained. He lifted his head, stared at Papa Bear for a few seconds, and then dropped his head back down.

"It's your time, Warrior." Papa Bear said to him and lifted him to his feet.

Papa Bear walked him out into the operating room. Then, with a powerful grip, he placed his hand around Ox's neck and forced him to lay down on the surgical table. Ox did not put up any struggle whatsoever.

Amil pressed a button on the wall, and a sixty-inch screen descended from the ceiling. She picked up a remote from a holster mounted to the wall and pointed it at the screen. Several close up photos of Fly from various angles appeared on the screen.

Ox was immediately given anesthesia, and the process began.

Chapter 8

As the weeks passed, Fly's stress level steadily increased. He'd been going back and forth from Rice Street to the Fulton county courthouse on blank trips. Some days, his case was just on the calendar. Other days, the state wasn't ready. They'd definitely built a strong, solid case with enough evidence to convict him. And one thing was for sure, Georgia wasn't about to let him plea out to insanity. They wanted his ass, and they were bringing everything they had to get the conviction.

Falisa was pulling strings and using her political connects from Florida. She'd hired two of the best attorneys that money could buy, just to make sure that her son was being represented properly. Fly's attorneys believed that the state was playing games, using the delays to pressure Fly into accepting a plea deal. The state had offered to take the death penalty off the table in exchange for life in prison with no possibility of parole. Fly's attorneys rejected that offer immediately.

Fly was in court again, dressed in a tailored three-piece suit and a crisp white shirt and gray tie. At the square defense table, a lawyer sat on each side of him; both dressed in power suits and sharp. The lawyer to his left was a slim white guy in his early forties with slick black hair and intelligent olive green eyes. His

Cole Hart

name was Antonio Day, straight out of Miami, Florida, where he'd beaten more than enough murder and federal drug cases.

The lawyer to his right, Richard Day, the younger brother of Antonio, was just as good and aggressive when it came to beating a case like this one. The brothers gained national attention three years ago by taking on a federal drug lord case out of Miami and winning in a jury trial. Amil had studied their case history, and had done a thorough background check on them. This was plan A. If the Day brothers managed to get Fly off, they would just find a different use for Ox.

Hours had passed. The state and the defense had carefully picked the jury that would determine if Fly would spend the rest of his days as a free man, as a state prisoner, or if he would have a life at all. On the other side of the courtroom, there was a high yellow woman who looked to be in her early fifties, with long flowing hair and strong cheekbones. She had sad eyes and a long stare that she kept fixed on the judge. Fly recognized her features, and instantly knew that she was Zoe's mother.

Fly turned away from her and leaned towards Richard on the right of him. "How much longer? I got to use the bathroom."

"A few more minutes," he whispered, and turned his attention back on the prosecutor who was blabbing off at the mouth about Fly being seventeen years old and a menace to society.

Now Fly was listening harder, his ears trained on the prosecutor as he was explaining to the court that Fly wasn't worth being in society. He was telling them that because he had expensive lawyers, and gold and diamonds in his mouth, that he was clearly a drug dealer. The prosecutor even went so far as to bring up his parents. He mentioned the fact that Fly was the son of notorious drug kingpin Timothy "Timbo" Walker, who had escaped federal custody and was still at large. He detailed the vast number of crimes, including murders that Timbo had been charged with. The prosecutor went on to say that, Falisa and Timbo had raised their children to be menaces to society and Fly was a clear example of their success.

At the mention of Falisa's name, Fly's head shot up. With a fierce scowl, he shook his head and pounded his fist into his open palm.

"Let him finish painting his picture, be cool." Antonio leaned over and said.

A month had passed since the surgery and Ox had healed evenly up to seventy percent. Amil sat with him nearly every day to make sure things were going as planned. They had given him facial implants that sized his cheekbones, chin and jaws the same diameter as Fly's features. Ox's nose had been a tad bit wider than Fly's nose at the bridge, and a little upturned. However, Aston was the best in the business and he'd fixed that also. He'd given him eyelid surgery and removed the few fingerprints that he did have. The biggest challenge was that they had to amputate Ox's leg. The same one that Fly was missing.

The Throne 3

Inside the small operating room, Amil wore jeans, Nikes and a white doctor's jacket over a blouse. Her hair was pulled back into a tight, neat ponytail. Papa Bear was with her. He brought Ox out of the small and uncomfortable room. He was sitting in a wheel chair, his leg was gone and his face was completely bandaged. They'd given him a large dosage of Haloperidol, commonly known as Haldol, which made it impossible for him to talk or to think straight. Ox was incoherent, nothing more than a shell.

When Amil removed his bandages, she was so impressed with Dr. Aston Oliver's work, she nearly cried. Seeing Ox look so much like Fly really drove home the reality of how much havoc she'd caused by sending her own brother to jail. Now she would make things right, with this amazing plan.

Papa Bear went to the left corner, where a brand new prosthesis was standing, still wrapped in plastic. He picked it up, tore the plastic from it, walked back over to Ox, and knelt down in front of him. He lifted Ox's face by placing a finger underneath his chin.

"Hey Warrior," he said softly. "How you doin?"

Ox looked at him; the Haldol had him slow and unsure of himself. Haldol is the drug used by the military during interrogations. It is prescribed for schizophrenia, but at a high dosage, it can turn a person into a zombie. Ox, of course, had been given the maximum dosage they could use without killing him.

When he didn't respond, Papa Bear strapped the prosthesis on his leg. "We got a week, soldier. One week, you'll be walking

Cole Hart   44

again, just like you never lost your leg." Papa Bear helped him to his feet.

Ox was wobbly; he didn't have a clue in the world as to what was going on. Papa Bear pulled Ox's arm and made him hug him around his neck.

"Let's walk. We gon' get you together, okay."

With a slow nod, Ox moved his lips. "Ok."

Amil stood to the side, taking one step at a time, slowly examining Ox's facial features. He looked almost exactly like her brother. Her eyes squinted, she took another step as he and Papa Bear took a step. *Seventy percent.* She said to herself.

"Now walk for me, Ox."

She watched him take another step, Papa Bear bracing him. Casually holding on to him like a toddler. Amil watched Papa Bear move directly in front of him. "Wait a minute." Papa said to Ox and took both of his hands in his. "Try walking by yourself."

Ox gazed blankly at Papa Bear, allowing his hands to rest comfortably inside of his. A look of fear crossed his face. Then he slowly shook his head. "It… hurt." he managed to say.

Mentally, Papa Bear felt his pain, but in his heart, he felt nothing but pure hatred. He was a coward, a heartless son of a bitch to kidnap an eleven-year-old child that Papa Bear loved as if she was his own.

The Throne 3

"It'll only hurt for a little while." He changed to a soft and kindhearted tone. "Then, I'll bless you." His head nodded forward.

Amil was standing four feet away, her arms folded across her chest. She watched Papa Bear turn on his charm and cracked a small smile. He amused her at times. She took a deep breath, and a moment later, Ox took his first step forward with his amputated leg. Amil's heart raced at that point. She watched Papa Bear release his hands and step back from Ox.

Ox held out his arms as if he was balancing himself. He moved his other leg, leaned to the left a little, then he straightened up and made another step. He extended his arms as if he was on a surfboard somewhere in the ocean. Papa Bear smiled, and out of his peripheral vision, he noticed that Amil was smiling from ear to ear.

When Papa Bear caught Amil staring at him, he winked his eye at her.

Chapter 9

The first week of the trial passed quickly. For three days, the prosecution methodically laid out their case against Fly. Witnesses, including the arresting officers, hotel personnel, and guests testified about what they saw on that terrible day. The state did an excellent job of portraying Fly as public enemy number one. The Day brothers did the best they could to counteract the damaging evidence and testimony, but it was an uphill journey.

On Friday morning, the prosecution put the final nail in Fly's coffin. They called Crime Scene Investigator, Andrew Nowalski from the Atlanta Police Department to the stand. Mr. Nowalski was sworn in, and the prosecutor wasted no time introducing the crime scene photos into evidence.

Gasps filled the courtroom as the gruesome photos of Zoe's shattered body appeared on the courtroom monitors. Fly glanced at the jury box, and even some of the men had tears in their eyes. Zoe's mother whimpered and ran out of the courtroom. At that moment, it hit him that he could possibly spend the rest of his life in prison. He prayed that his mother would be able to work a miracle for him.

Cole Hart

Investigator Nowalski took the jury through several photos, showing the horror that Zoe experienced when she was tossed thirty-three stories to her death. Her head exploded on impact and her contorted body resembled that of a rag doll. The photos had the desired effect; the sorrow and revulsion in the air was almost palpable.

Fly dropped his head in his hands, the weight of the situation bearing down on him.

After Nowalski's damaging testimony, the prosecution rested. The judge announced that court would resume on Monday morning, when the defense would present its case.

As they stood for the judge's departure, Antonio whispered in Fly's ear. "Tomorrow, go to medical and request to have your gold teeth removed. Don't ask me why, just do it. It's your mother's decision."

Fly turned and looked the attorney dead in his eyes to ensure that he was hearing him correctly. Antonio bowed his head slightly. His eyes were soothing as if he knew something more than Fly.

By 7:48 that evening, Fly was back in his cell on Rice Street, talking to Falisa on the phone. "Tomorrow is Saturday, Mama, and I don't think the dentist dude comes in on the weekend."

"He'll be there. Just make sure you do as you're told. If we don't do it this weekend, it can't be done. We have to do this before your trial starts back on Monday."

"Alright, I'll do that first thing in the morning."

"And Fly," Amil said from the other end.

"Yeah."

"Make sure you keep your gold teeth."

The following morning at 9:00 am, Fly was escorted downstairs to a small nurse's station that led around a corridor to a small doctor office. The fresh scent of bleach was in his nostrils. He wasn't in his wheelchair this morning, and was walking pretty well on his prosthesis. A Fulton county deputy sheriff waited outside the small office while Fly stepped inside.

The dentist was a short white guy in khaki pants and white overcoat. He wore wire frame glasses. His face was fleshy and his neck was thick. He stood face to face with Fly and extended his hand out to him.

Fly shook his hand.

"Good morning," the dentist greeted Fly.

Fly bowed his head slightly, "Morning."

The dentist guided Fly to a thick wooden door and went through it. Inside the room was a leather dentist chair. The walls were painted white and there were florescent lights that gave the small four-corner room a bright glare.

"Have a seat." he told Fly and pointed to the chair.

Fly climbed into the cushioned seat. He scanned the office, really wondering what the hell was going on. Falisa had refused to give him any details, insisting that he follow her directions without question. Fly hated being left in the dark, but this time, he didn't argue. Every time he failed to listen to his mother in the past, he had paid dearly. A missing leg, three years in a Columbian jail, and his current predicament was enough to teach anyone a lesson.

Fly laid back and relaxed, now staring up toward the ceiling. The dentist was to his left, preparing his utensils and materials to remove Fly's gold teeth from his mouth. In less than an hour, he'd removed them and cleaned Fly's original teeth and polished them white.

He handed Fly a mirror to look at himself. He spread his lips and examined his teeth in the reflection. Then the dentist guy handed Fly a small Ziploc bag with eight gold caps embedded with diamonds. He looked at them and balled them up in the palm of his hand.

"I don't like the way my teeth look." Fly said to him.

"I'm sure you'll upgrade once you get out," the dentist said as he handed Fly two small tubes of crazy glue.

Now why is this dude giving me crazy glue? Fly questioned silently.

Fly asked him what it was for, but the dentist just shrugged, and said, "I'm just following instructions, Mr. Walker."

Later that day, Fly visited the nurse to get some pain meds for his sore mouth. She gave him a small pouch, which he secured in his pants. He thanked her and left with the guard.

Back in his cell, Fly sat on his bed, studying the contents of the pouch. There was a note from Falisa, a pair of scissors, a hair net, four small vials of a clear liquid, and a pack of ten insulin needles. Fly couldn't help but to smile as he read the letter from his mother. She was truly the queen.

Chapter 10

It was 4:00 am, and windy. The sky was dark and cloudy in Atlanta, Georgia. Papa Bear and Pig Man were in a flatbed truck with a glossy black Porsche 911 on the rear. Papa Bear was behind the wheel and Pig Man was on the passenger side. They pulled up on Rice Street and parked two blocks away from the county jail. Pig Man and Papa Bear stepped down together.

Papa Bear climbed up on the rear of the flatbed, cautiously looking in both directions to make sure no Fulton County police cars were creeping by. Papa Bear went to the passenger side of the Porsche, opened the door, and got inside. To his left, Ox was sitting in the driver seat, carefully strapped in his seatbelt. He was leaning; his head pressed against the window and saliva was seeping from the corner of his mouth. He was drugged to the point that he didn't know his name, let alone where he was.

Papa Bear checked his pulse; it was thumping. Then he pulled out a small half a pint of Seagram's Gin, held his mouth open, and poured some down his throat. Ox began to choke on the liquor, so he poured the rest on his shirt and between his legs.

Papa Bear topped the bottle, opened the door, and stepped out. Afterwards, Pig Man clicked a few switches and the flatbed tilted up at an angle, then they removed the Porsche 911 and left it parked neatly against the curb, with Ox behind the wheel.

Papa Bear then went around to the driver side and slightly opened the door, so that the interior light shone into the night.

After Papa Bear and Pig Man pulled off, Pig Man made a direct call to a crooked Fulton county officer that they had on their payroll.

The crooked officer, who was out with his partner, smoothly turned down Rice Street and spotted the Porsche by its illuminated interior light. "Check it out," he said, as they got closer to the Porsche.

"Damn, someone is in there. He doesn't look conscious. Let's go see what's up." His partner suggested.

"Yeah, might as well, since we're here," the crooked officer agreed.

They pulled up alongside the Porsche and switched on the blue lights. The crooked officer threw the car in park and got out. When he walked around to the driver side window, he put the flashlight in the face of the inebriated driver. His partner peered into the passenger side window.

The officer opened the door, and Ox tilted toward him. The smell of alcohol filled his nostrils. "Hey, my man." The officer said.

Ox didn't respond.

"Hey man, are you ok? This isn't the best place to take a nap." The officer's partner said, as he opened the passenger door.

Ox briefly looked at them blankly, and then nodded off again.

The officers pulled Ox from the Porsche and patted him down. Finding nothing on him, the partner half carried him to the squad car. The crooked officer stayed at the Porsche under the guise of looking for registration or ID.

He opened the glove compartment, where the keys to the Porsche were. He discreetly made a call. "We're on our way in," he said.

"Good. Everything is ready here. Hurry up."

The officer returned to the squad car, with the keys to the Porsche in his pocket. He informed his partner that there was no registration or ID in the car. They agreed to just get him to the station and let the drunk worry about his own vehicle when he sobered up. They shared a laugh at the fact that money obviously doesn't buy common sense.

Ox was delivered to the county jail, where he was charged with only simple public intoxication. Due to their inside connections, he was not booked. Instead, they placed him inside a holding tank where he would sleep off his drunkenness. However, no more than two hours later, they moved him upstairs to the third floor, when he started to convulse from what they thought was the alcohol leaving his system. In reality, the convulsions were a side effect of the Haldol. Because of his missing leg, they thought it was best not to take a chance on him falling from the narrow cot in the drunk tank and injuring himself.

He was transferred to the medical floor, the exact same dorm where Fly was waiting on him. Fly had followed Falisa's instructions to the T and had cut his dreads off. The old man had glued Fly's dreads to the hair net and made a wig full of dreads. Ox was in the cell next door to Fly and the old man. As soon as the coast was clear, they crept into Ox's cell for the most crucial phase of the plan.

Fly injected Ox with another dose of the Haldol, mixed with Lithium. This ensured that Ox would be out of it long enough for them to do their work. The old man glued the dread wig onto Ox's head, while Fly crazy glued his old and used gold teeth that he'd had removed into Ox's mouth.

After they finished the makeover, they took a moment to admire their handiwork. "Dammit boy, if that nigga don't look like you, I don't know who does. I know one thing. I'm sho glad to be on your good side, and not the other way around. You muthafuckas don't play." The old man whispered.

Fly chuckled and said, "I appreciate you, old timer. Whatever you need, whenever you need it, I got you. But enough of this talking. Let's finish this shit, before they start coming around for the count, or someone comes to check on this nigga."

Fly switched inmate ID bands with Ox. He was elated at the thought of getting out of that hellhole. He was even more pleased with the fact that another one of his enemies would be getting what they deserve.

The Throne 3

The old man checked the hall. It was still dark and quiet in the early morning hours. They put Ox in Fly's wheelchair and quietly rolled him next door to the cell that Fly had shared with the old man. After they got Ox in the bed, Fly and the old man said their goodbyes.

Fly repeated his promise to look out for him, and without another word, he left his cell and went next door to where Ox had been kept.

When it was time for Fly to go to court, they would take Ox instead. He would have to answer for Fly's sins for the rest of little life he had left. The combination of Haldol and Lithium would keep him groggy and cooperative, and once Fly was safe, the old man would deliver the final lethal dose that would stop his heart.

Two hours later, Fly was released on his own recognizance, and left Fulton county jail without a problem. He walked to the end of the block and turned the corner. He spotted the waiting Porsche 911 and smiled. He picked up his pace as he walked across the street to the car and retrieved the key from the metal box under the spoiler.

Once in the car, he took a deep breath, inhaling the luxurious aroma of fine leather. He started the car and winked at his reflection in the rearview mirror. "The ruler is back."

Chapter 11

On Monday morning, the courtroom was crowded. The media had a field day with the dramatic conclusion of Friday's court session, and people could not wait to see what the defense had put together.

When the defendant was wheeled into the courtroom, he didn't look like his usual self. He wore his dreads loose and wild, and his eyes held a vacant glare. Dressed in his expensive suit, he looked at the judge, staring blankly. His eyes went down to the floor and back up to the white female court reporter. He explored her body with his eyes. She was dressed in a cheap polyester blouse that was tucked into the waistline of a blue skirt. His gave finally rested on her legs, continuing to stare as if he was captivated.

When she caught him staring, she leaned over and whispered something in the bailiff's ear.

The bailiff walked over and stood before him and the two lawyers. He leaned down and whispered, "Mr. Walker is something wrong with your eyes?"

The Throne 3

There was no response. He didn't even look up at the bailiff. Saliva had settled in the corner of his mouth, and when it began to leak, he slowly caught it with the back of his hand. The bailiff snapped his fingers, and the loud sound made the young man look up. The disheveled young man stared into his eyes and didn't flinch one time. Then unexpectedly, he began shaking his head violently from side-to-side. His dreads were swinging and slapping across the face of the lawyer, Antonio.

The lawyer grabbed his client by his shoulders and pulled him close to calm him down. "Just relax." He whispered.

His eyes continued to stare blankly as if he'd slipped into his own little world. The attorney looked up at the bailiff and said, "Everything is fine, sir. He's under control."

Without another word, the bailiff turned on his heels and walked back across the courtroom. He stood next to the court reporter and stared in their direction.

When the judge entered, the bailiff shouted, "All rise."

The judge climbed the small flight of stairs to take his place at the bench. He was brown skinned with a beard, and wore glasses. When he scanned the courtroom, he caught a glimpse of the boy sitting in his wheelchair at the defense table. His index finger was deep up his nose. *What a disgusting sight,* he thought. *He really has no respect for the court. Who raised this animal? If his little crazy act is a buildup for an insanity defense, he'd better think again. This monster will not walk the streets, not on my watch.* He slowly shook his head and announced to the courtroom that they could be seated.

The sound of shuffling feet and chatter filled the air as everyone took their seats. Then, within seconds, the entire courtroom turned silent. The judge took his seat, looked around again and caught Fly and his attorney whispering to each other.

The judge cleared his throat.

Richard Day looked up at the judge and stood up. "Your honor, my client is ready to take a plea deal."

Surprised murmurs rippled through the courtroom. The jurors seemed to be in shock.

The tall, slim district attorney stood up. "Your honor, this is highly irregular." The young DA said. He tried to maintain his chagrined look, but secretly, he was delighted by the new development. *An easy conviction,* he thought to himself. He was confident in his case, but was more than a little intimidated by the famous Day brothers. Their record of acquittals was legendary.

The judge finally rapped his gavel against the small circular piece of wood. "Order!" He yelled out. He scowled at the room, menacingly, to show that he was indeed angry. He made eye contact with the DA. They both were hoping that they had heard correctly.

"Permission to approach the bench?" Richard said.

"Granted." The judge replied. "Both of you."

The two attorneys walked up to the judge's bench together and began whispering amongst the three of them. "He wants the plea?" the judge asked,

The Throne 3

After a deep breath, Richard nodded his head. "We're taking a plea."

The DA looked at him. "Life without the possibility of parole, and nothing less. Our terms have not changed."

The judge looked at the DA. "Do you have your original papers in court with you?"

"Yes sir."

"Very well, then. I have no objection, as long as the defendant signs."

The men returned to their tables. The judge asked the young man if he was changing his plea to guilty.

"Sure, why not?" he said, and then collapsed into a fit of laughter. He seemed to find the whole thing hilarious.

Frustrated, the judge barked, "Yes or No!"

"Yes."

The D.A. chuckled and hurried over to the defense table with the papers.

Antonio gave him an ink pen and whispered in his ear, "Your name is Derrick Walker."

He seemed confused for a second, and then he shrugged and smiled, flashing a bunch of raggedy looking gold teeth that were in the front of his mouth. He wrote his name to the best of his ability, drawing the letters like a first grader. Derrick Walker.

Cole Hart

60

Cole Hart

Chapter 12

Quantico, Virginia

From his small motel-like room, he stood in the window, staring out at the view he'd had of the forest. It was raining and very cold outside. The bulletproof window was streaked with rainwater. It was 3:05 a.m. and Six was up. He stared carefully toward the dark gray clouds, lost in his own thoughts, replaying his life and the drastic turn that it had taken in the last few months. Just the thought of it made him sick to his stomach, as if he'd drank a gallon of spoiled milk.

He took a deep breath, then another one, his chest rising and falling, shifting the weight if his body from one foot to the other one. He turned away from the window and looked around the small one bedroom where he was hiding out in protective custody. Dressed in a pair of denim jeans and a T-shirt, his shoes were neatly parked on the side of his queen-sized bed.

Six sat down at the foot of the bed. He fell backwards, with his hands behind his head, and stared blankly at the ceiling. He didn't see the hidden camera, but the hidden camera definitely saw him. He dug in his nose, rolled the booger into a ball, and then thumped it across the room. His life was on the line, but at this particular moment, he was already dead to the city of Augusta.

He thought back to the morning his mother came down to the county jail to visit him. He envisioned Papa Bear standing downstairs, leaning on the front bumper of the SUV with his shiny harmonica in his hand. The cold, chilling message that his mother had delivered to him still rang in his ears. *They said if they don't read about you in the morning newspaper, that they'll make sho' you read about us.* Those words would never leave Six's memory. That wasn't something not easily forgotten.

Six squeezed his eyes shut. He wanted this all to go away. Disappear like a David Copperfield magic trick. He grinded down hard on his back teeth. Smurf wanted him dead, but he wasn't going to go out like that. He had almost gave in, the threat to his mother and grandmother had crushed him. He was willing to sacrifice his life to save them, but thankfully, he was rescued from that fate. Just as he was about to take his life, a guard came in and took him to meet with federal agents. They were aware of the situation and presented him with an alternative.

As Six reminisced, he couldn't help but to think that the man upstairs was looking out for him. Five minutes later, and the news reports would've been true. Now, he was determined; he surely wasn't about to go to prison, not with all the information he had to offer.

He got up, walked back to the window and stared blankly. *I'll have to leave the United States,* he said to himself. But where could I go? Papa Bear popped into his head. He saw the old man, his wide shoulders and long powerful arms. His cold and deadly

Cole Hart

stare, then he went further into his memory bank and thought about how he was sitting on the curb in the projects pretending to be a bum and playing his harmonica. That gave him a chill. Six feared Papa Bear for several reasons, but mainly because he'd seen him work.

One hour passed, and it was a little after four a.m. Six was becoming even more nervous. At 5:00 a.m., a knock came from the other side of his room door, and then it came open. A head peeped inside; it was a white guy with gray hair, a fat nose, and a square chin. He came all the way in, dressed in a two-piece blue suit and a crisp white shirt.

"Good morning."

Six stood up and walked towards the door where he stood. "Good morning."

"This morning, you'll be meeting with Agent Jennings. He's the agent in charge of the unsolved homicides at MCG Hospital. We'll go in here and sit at the table. You'll be asked some questions. Just answer them truthfully, and you'll be okay."

Six swallowed. He was now worried and it showed on his face. He took a deep breath, desperately trying to get himself together. He walked toward the bed and eased his feet into his shoes, one foot at a time. Finally, he followed the federal agent out the room and into a narrow corridor. They went toward one of the three elevators and entered. Six was so nervous that he nearly passed gas on the elevator.

When the doors rolled open, there were two more federal agents waiting in the carpeted corridor. A male and a female. Neither of them greeted Six at all and only shook hands with their fellow agent. When they got to the conference room, Six looked around and noticed that the room was windowless and the ceiling was low. A long, polished oak table held ten leather cushioned chairs. Four chairs on each side, facing each other and a chair at each end. Four of the chairs were already occupied with federal agents. The men all wore suits and the female agents were in skirts, low heels and crisp white blouses.

When Six was pointed to the available seat, he sat down next to a black guy. Special Agent Jennings had light skin features and his curly hair swept toward the back. He gave Six his hand and brought up a briefcase from underneath the table. He popped open the brass latches, flipped it open, and removed a stack of file folders.

"Good morning." Six finally responded nervously. He noticed that the three agents who escorted him to the room never took a seat.

Agent Jennings stared at Six briefly. The other agents looked at him also, studying his body language. They knew he was scared, it showed in his eyes.

"Tell us a little something about yourself," one of the agents said to Six.

Six took a deep breath. He felt sweat around his neck, running down the center of his chest.

Cole Hart

Before he could speak, one of the female agents slid her elbows upon the table and placed her hands underneath her chin. "Let's cut the bullshit," she said. "This is an organized-crime case and you're the star witness. We don't normally fake deaths for anyone unless it's mafia status. So, first things, first..." She paused, opened a manila envelope and removed a few eight-by-ten color photographs that had been cropped and blown up. She slid them across the table to Six, and he saw the image of the girl shot to death in her hospital bed at MCG Hospital. "What can you tell us about her?"

"Far as I know, she was supposed to be testifying against Timbo..."

"Timbo. That's Timothy Timbo Walker, correct?"

"Yes."

Pens and paper came out, small tape recorders clicked on, and everyone began taking notes and listening intently.

"And how were you involved with this murder?"

"Well, Timbo ordered the hit, and he ordered his son to do it. My friend, Smurf, and I were in on it. I drove the getaway car. Smurf and Fly went into the hospital dressed like a clown and a candy striper."

Agent Jennings studied some notes and old files he had from 1993, when the case happened. *So far, so good,* he thought to himself. His eyes went to Six. "Did you ever meet the infamous Timbo?"

Six shook his head. "No sir."

Do you know where he's hiding? Has anyone seen him?"

All eyes were trained on Six. Sweat began pouring from his face and he wiped his forehead with the back of his hand. His eyes darted around the room, looking each agent in their eyes. Another long, deep breath, then he said, "Yeah, he's dead."

Calmly, another agent asked, "Are you sure of this? How do you know?"

"I watched him die. I even know where he's buried. But before I go any further, I wanna go to Canada to live, and have my mother and grandmother come with me." His eyes searched the room, waiting for an answer.

Silence permeated the air and hung heavy like a wet blanket.

The older, gray haired director finally spoke up. "I'm sure we can arrange that."

Six broke into a smile. He cleared his throat and began talking, like his mouth had diarrhea.

Chapter 13

After Fly was freed, Falisa immediately sent for him and ordered a family meeting at the all-white mansion in Miami. Fly was dressed in expensive denim jeans, a thousand dollar Lanvin t-shirt, and Jordans. His do it yourself county haircut had been shaped into a low Caesar. Smurf was in the rear of the limousine, sitting next to him, but his focus was outside of the car. He stared out the dark tint window and watched the blazing lights from the city skyline as they rode in pure silence.

Sipping on a glass of Hennessy and no chaser, he finally looked over and studied Fly. Fly caught his stare; his facial expression was serious. They looked each other square in the eye until Smurf finally cracked a grin. His golds and diamonds sparkled underneath the limousine's interior lighting.

Smurf turned up the glass of Hennessy and didn't turn it down until the glass was empty. "On some real shit, I don't know how the hell Amil and Falisa came up wit' the plan to get you out." He paused and moved his dreads from his eyes. Smurf smiled at fly, reached into the leather compartment, and removed a wooden box filled with fresh Cuban cigars. He offered Fly one, and he took it.

Fly examined the cigar. A smile reappeared. Then he turned his head toward the window and looked at the illuminated skyline of Miami. "I know that Hawk is down here somewhere, Smurf." He spoke in a soft, dangerous tone. "I don't give a fuck where I see that nigga at. It's on sight."

Smurf pulled out a lighter, struck it and held the flame at the tip of his cigar. His eyes were trained on Fly. "You don't have to worry about seeing him. Niggas like that ain't in our circle." He lit the cigar and puffed until smoke outlined his face. "We got Learjet money, and it's still growing, lil brah." Then he gave Fly the lighter.

"Man, I don't smoke no cigars."

Smurf leaned closer to him, removed his cigar from his mouth, and said to Fly, "Power moves like this is cause for a celebration." He shoved the lighter in his face.

Fly hesitated for a few seconds, and then he took it and lit his own cigar. He began coughing and fanning the smoke. The taste was sweet, and relaxed his mouth to accept the exquisite taste.

The limousine slowed down. Smurf's eyes shifted to the window and noticed that they were pulling toward the entrance gate of the all-white mansion. There were two high tech surveillance cameras mounted on concrete pillars on each side of the long driveway. The twelve-foot iron gates rolled open, and the limousine proceeded further. The gates closed behind them and they moved up toward the mansion and parked in the circular part of the driveway.

When the limousine finally came to a complete stop, the driver stepped out, walked around and opened the rear door. The cigar smoke seeped out first, and then Fly stepped out. He was depending on his cane this evening. His cigar pressed between two fingers, he made a circle and waited for Smurf to step out. The ocean breeze ruffled his thousand-dollar t-shirt.

Smurf got out, and they fell in stride together and walked up to the huge front door. Before they knocked, someone pulled it open. They were face to face with Pepé.

A smile appeared on Pepé's face when he saw Fly. "You made it." He said in heavily accented English. He extended his hand out to Fly. "We no smoke in here. Your mother, lungs not good."

Smurf immediately snubbed out his cigar and Fly did the same. They followed Pepé inside. Fly watched Pepé from the back. Just by his demeanor and the way he walked, money exuded from him. He always wore expensive clothing and jewelry, and he kept himself clean. As he walked, his hard bottom dress shoes clicked across the marble tile.

Inside the high ceilinged living room, the walls were covered with a cream-colored fabric. Two crystal chandeliers hung; one in the west corner and the other one in the east corner. Pepé led Fly and Smurf through a narrow corridor, then toward a wooden door. Pepé opened the door. Inside, the room was spacious and tastefully decorated with expensive paintings, double stuffed sofas, and loveseats. The four leather chairs were imported from a store in Brazil. There was a four feet high fireplace built into the wall, with two additional chairs facing it.

Falisa sat alone in one of those chairs, staring at the small flames. Fly walked around the chair and stood in front of her. She looked up at him and her eyes moisten at the sight of her son.

Without a word, he leaned down, hugged her, and kissed her cheek. "Thank you," he whispered.

"You don't have to thank me," she replied in a whisper.

Fly took her hand in his, brought it up to his mouth and kissed the back of it. He sat down in the available chair next to her. Smurf then came around and gave Falisa a warm embrace.

He took her hand and kissed the back of it. "How you feeling?" he asked her.

She bowed her head. "I'm fair. Not quite excellent yet, but I'm working on it."

Smurf patted her hand politely. She stared up at him. "Give us a few minutes."

He went toward the door. Pepé walked over to Falisa, slightly bent at the waist and kissed her cheek. He straightened back up, and walked out, closing the door behind him. That left Fly and Falisa in the room alone.

Falisa stared into the flames, and then she turned her head and looked at her son for a brief moment, and then turned back toward the flames. Her voice came low, but her words were strong and powerful. "Allow me to apologize to you first. I took it upon myself to baby you when I found out that Zoe was full of betrayal. I called myself helping you by helping her. I'll always try to make it my business that my kids are at their best. So it was bad judgment on my part."

Fly watched Falisa. His focus was strictly on her, and he listened closely to her every word. Then he said, "Well, the only problem I got with this whole situation is that my sistah is playing offense against me. That shouldn't happen if we're on the same team."

There was a long silence between the two of them.

"On my word," Falisa whispered. Her head turned toward him. "Amil will be forever loyal to you and everyone else. I know deep down inside it's hard for you to believe that. However, she is the one responsible for your being here today. And I mean it. From here on, she's ready." she took a breath. "You got your position back as long as you stay focused on the business. Amil will assist you, if it's not a problem."

Fly's eyes studied Falisa for a brief moment. He looked into the fireplace and quickly looked back at Falisa. "So we'll share the Throne?" he asked her, his question came easy, however his words were powerful.

"That's the way I want it, Fly."

Fly stood up, using his cane as leverage. He walked over to Falisa and stood in front of her. Falisa looked up at him. He reached for her hand and when he got it, he pulled her just enough to let her know that he wanted her to stand up. Falisa rose to her feet, and for the first time she actually saw that he'd gotten taller.

"I don't want to bury my children… I'd prefer my children bury me."

Fly kissed his mother's forehead, his eyes closed briefly. Then he opened them and his heart rate accelerated. "I'll make sure I handle the family business. I'm ready, and if you're cosigning for Amil, I will not go against your word or judgment again." He finally embraced his mother and held on to her.

She whispered in his ear, "You're a king. Act like one."

Falisa sat back down while Fly continued to stand directly in front of her. She grabbed his hand, carefully massaged from his wrist down to his fingers. Then she eased it up to her lips and kissed the back of it.

Chapter 14

When Fly separated from Falisa, he went out into the hallway and made a right. Two doors down was a guest room; the door was slightly ajar and soft music was playing inside. Fly didn't want to be nosey, but he peeked his head inside anyway. He saw Iris standing in front of a wall mirror. She saw him in the reflection and simply said, "Come in, please."

Fly stepped inside the tastefully furnished bedroom and closed the door behind him. When he walked over toward Iris, he noticed that her ass and breasts were much bigger and her hips and thighs were firmer and thick. She was in a halter top and boy shorts. "Where you get all that ass from?" Fly asked her, half-jokingly.

Iris hugged him, and then she slowly backed away from him and looked him up and down. A smile adorned her pretty face. She grabbed both of his hands and placed them on her ass. "You like it?" she asked him.

Fly gripped her ass cheeks. They were soft in his hands. He pulled her close and sniffed her neck. She smelled like freshly cut roses. He planted a soft kiss below her ear. "Feels real good."

Iris pressed against him. She could feel him growing hard in his jeans. She kissed his lips. "Let me take you in the bathroom." Her tongue slipped inside his mouth. "And bathe you."

She led Fly into a huge bathroom. The floor was made of marble tile that led up to a spacious black Jacuzzi. She filled the tub with steaming hot water. Fly looked at himself in the mirror while Iris got completely naked behind him. As she rolled her boy shorts down her legs, Fly turned around and examined her entire body. The surgeon had definitely worked a miracle. The last time he'd seen her, she was nearly skin and bones. Now her body was sculpted and defined like an old Coca Cola bottle.

Fly leaned against the vanity, his hands were stacked atop each other, and his bottom hand was holding his cane. Iris walked up to him. She rubbed both hands all over his head. "You're seventeen now. That means you're grown. I think your new look is sexy."

Fly smiled, sat his cane to the side and cupped her ass cheeks again. He pulled her even closer and touched the wetness of her vagina from the back.

She tensed, then she whispered, "It's all for you."

After the Jacuzzi was full, she waited for Fly to remove his prosthesis and his clothes, and then led him into the hot water. Iris bathed him from head to toe, then she mounted him and grinded slowly, riding him with a rhythm that caused the pace of his heart to speed up. Fly sucked her nipples as she threw her head back and closed her eyes.

Cole Hart

Fly's hands nearly wrapped around her small waist, and he pushed his rock hard penis further up into her tight vaginal walls. He pulled her face down to his and kissed her cheeks, one at a time.

She moaned and rode harder. "Are you gonna cum in me?"

His pulse raced with each thrust. He was so hard, he felt as if his penis was about to erupt. "What if my son comes out with one leg?"

She laughed, nearly breaking her concentration. "You're always joking. Are you gonna ever be serious?"

"I'm about to cum."

Iris rode him harder. He pushed deeper and they came together.

An hour later, Fly was in another part of the mansion, a huge room upstairs that overlooked the ocean. Inside this room was an octagon shaped bar on the left wall. Papa Bear stood behind the glossy wood bar, wiping out the crystal glasses. This was Fly's first time seeing Papa since he'd been out. Fly walked toward the bar and Papa came from around the rear, a joyous expression on his face.

Papa hugged Fly, swallowed him up in his powerful arms. Then he pulled back and stared him in his eyes. "Plain and simple, Fly. When you're given wise words, take them for what their worth."

Fly's smile faded as he looked up into Papa Bear's eyes. He listened to him very carefully, at the same time, thinking about all the mistakes that he'd made. Papa Bear had a hand on each of Fly shoulders. Fly nodded his head in agreement then Papa Bear hugged him again. They headed across the huge and spacious room where Smurf and Pig Man were standing over a billiards table. Pig Man had the shot, slightly bent at the waist, carefully pulling, and pushing his cue stick toward the cue ball. He had one eye closed, measuring his shot.

He whispered to Smurf, "Twelve ball, corna pocket." He pushed the stick, not too much force. He sunk the twelve ball with ease and then stood up. He looked at Fly with a smile. "You got to be a menace to society. Far worse than O dawg." He shook his head and walked around the table to where Fly stood. He put his arm around his neck. "Let me tell you something," he said, "yo' muthafuckin' sistah is a pure genius."

"So I'm hearing."

"No, you don't hear what I'm saying." Pig Man leaned his stick against the table, and the four of them sat down, everyone finding their own comfortable seat. "Listen at me closely when I tell you this," Pig Man said. "Yo ass would be still behind bars if it wasn't for her. This whole plan was her idea. I'm talking about from start to finish, every detail was hers."

"Yeah man, I just wonder what it'll cost me." Fly said and shook his head. "Where is she?" He turned to Papa Bear. They stared at each other for a brief moment.

Papa Bear said in slow, deep tone. "She's scared to face you."

Cole Hart

"For what? We settled our differences over the phone." Fly said.

"She still feels uneasy about the situation," Papa Bear said calmly.

He stood up and stretched, and then he walked over toward Fly and stood over him. He reached for Fly. Fly stood up as well, and Papa bear put his arm around his neck. They turned around and walked out of the room and into the hallway where the huge mansion was quiet. Papa looked down at Fly. The soft lights shone down over his face. He rested his huge hands on each of Fly's shoulders.

"Do you believe in me?" Papa Bear asked him, his deadly eyes staring directly into Fly's eyes.

Fly's eyes narrowed, but he never flinched nor turned away from Papa Bear. Then he moved his head up and down like an obedient little boy. "Without a doubt," Fly shot back.

"Good." he said and turned left, away from Fly. "Follow me." He walked further down the hallway, bypassing wooden doors and classical paintings. The hall opened up to a huge sitting room that was tastefully furnished. Through that room, they moved up a short flight of stairs that led them toward the rear of the mansion. There was a door on the right. Papa stopped there and knocked on it softly.

There was no answer, but he could hear footsteps on the other side then her soft voice. "Yes"

"It's me, Papa. I got your brother with me."

Cole Hart 78

Fly had subconsciously moved behind Papa Bear. His eyes were on the door when it cracked open. It squeaked on its hinges when she opened it all the way. They stared at each other long and hard. Her face was soft and her eyes were innocent, her hair was pulled back and her body had fully developed.

Fly eased up to her. She opened the door wider and came out. Papa Bear stepped to the side and allowed them to enjoy the moment. Fly reached out for her, and when she walked into his arms, she began crying. Her arms wrapped around him tightly. "I'm sorry, Fly." she said in a muffled tone.

Fly kissed her forehead, wrapped his arms around her neck and shoulders and squeezed her firmly. "Do you know how much I love you?" he asked her.

Without a word, she just relaxed in her brother's arms. She felt comfortable as a sleeping baby as tears still streaked her face. "I know." she finally whispered. "And I love you too, I promise I do."

Fly could feel her shaking in his arms. He kissed her cheek. "Why you shaking?" he whispered.

She shrugged, but she was nervous. She took a deep breath and desperately tried to calm down. "I just want us to be right." She lifted her head and looked at Papa Bear. He smiled at her and slowly nodded his head with pure satisfaction.

"We gonna talk." she said to him.

"Y'all go ahead, take your time." He stepped up and wrapped his long massive arms around both of them in one big group hug.

Cole Hart

He kissed them both on top of their heads and walked away. "I'll be in the kitchen."

Fly and Amil went through the doors and Fly closed it behind him. The room was low and very comfortable looking. The walls were made of expensive wood and thick wall-to-wall carpet. There was no furniture, just a bunch of overstuffed pillows on the floor and a wooden desk with a computer on top.

Fly looked around. "Whose room is this?"

Amil grabbed his hand and pulled him toward the stack of pillows that were on the floor. "This is my think tank," she said. "I spend a lot of time here." She released his hand and playfully fell backwards and allowed her pillows to catch her.

Fly dropped down onto the pillows also; they were soft and comfortable. They sat quietly for the next ten minutes. Fly had his hands behind his head, staring up toward the ceiling. Amil was laying on her back, staring at the ceiling also. They could hear each other breathing. Then finally, she asked, "Are you gonna let me work with you?"

Fly broke into a smile, and then he slowly turned his head to look at her. "What is it that you're looking for?"

"Whatever, I just want to help you protect the Throne."

Fly sat silently for the next three minutes. He knew Amil was growing up quickly. She'd been through so much. He thought all the way back to when she was kidnapped, and even to this day, that still made his flesh crawl. Hawk jumped back into his head and his heart turned cold all over again. Fly leaned over towards

Cole Hart

her, held his pinky finger up. She looked at him and locked her pinky around his. "Make me a promise," he said.

"Okay."

He stared at her; she stared back. Their hearts were beating in unison. "If anything happens to me, make sho' Pepé's body is never found."

"I promise." she whispered. Then she said, "Why? I thought he was alright."

Fly hesitated briefly, then took a deep breath and told her the situation.

Chapter 15

Six was more comfortable now than he was a few weeks ago. Still living his life in hiding, still in protective custody, still in Quantico, Virginia. Today, he was in the cafeteria with a female federal agent who was pale and simple looking. Together, they occupied a square table, sitting across from each other. Six was eating steamed broccoli, sautéed wild salmon and mini stuffed mushrooms. He'd gained some confidence, and was now less worried than he'd been a few weeks ago. He had picked up a little weight and it showed in his face.

With a mouth full of food, he looked up at the agent. Her skin was pale, and desperately in need of a tan. She was dressed in an off-white blouse that was tucked in the waistline of her blue skirt. She sipped ice tea from a straw and Styrofoam cup. Her eyes were sharp and alert, and staring dead at him. They still had Six under scrutiny; they wanted everything he had to offer. No rocks left unturned.

She carefully sat her cup down and eased her elbows on the table. "How's the food?" she asked him, not smiling.

Six nodded while chewing vigorously, then he picked up his own cup of ice tea, took three long gulps, and sat the cup back down. His eyes went to hers. "Food is wonderful here. Better than

McDonalds." he said and picked up a mini mushroom and threw it into his mouth. Then he asked. "You ain't eating?"

She smiled. Her teeth were stained with coffee. "I'm watching my weight." Her smile faded and she changed the subject. Her facial expression was unreadable. "Is there anything else that you can think of? Something of value to us and to you?"

Six sat still, the wheels began turning in his mind, he was thinking hard. He'd basically told them everything that he knew and had testified in front of a federal grand jury. But most of his testimony was hearsay, because he didn't know everything about Falisa and Papa Bear. His eyes shifted from the table and up to hers. "Did y'all ever find Fly?"

"Derrick Walker, aka Fly. Yes, he pled guilty to a gruesome murder down in Atlanta Georgia. He's no good to us."

"No good?" Six nearly shouted, his eyebrows bunching together with a look of confusion on his face.

She shook her head slowly, picked up her cup again and sipped from her straw. "He died last week in Fulton county jail."

"From what?"

"Don't know, don't care. They said his heart stopped or something."

Six blew out a long drawn out breath, as if he'd been defeated. Silence hung in the air between the two of them. He couldn't believe that Fly was dead. That was a devastating blow. "Is this a fact or did somebody tell you this?" His eyes went down to his food. He'd lost his appetite, just that quick.

She shrugged. "Trust me, he's dead."

Six rubbed the short beard underneath his chin and tilted his head back, looking toward the ceiling, thinking harder than before. He finally brought his head back down and looked her dead in her eyes. "Only thing I can think of is Papa Bear's Farm. I'm still tryin' to figure out why ya'll haven't gone down there yet." His tone of voice was low.

The lady leaned in, and whispered, "You're not an agent, just an informant. We focus on solid concrete information that'll give us an entire organization. Is that understood?"

Six sat still, his eyes fixed on hers. Then he picked up his fork and cut into his wild salmon that was quickly turning cold. "Did I tell ya'll about Iris?" he carefully eased the piece of fish into his mouth.

Her eyebrows rose. "Iris? No, who is this?"

"All I know is that Iris is some chick from Washington D.C that was on Americas Most Wanted."

The agent pulled out a cell phone and speed dialed a number. For the next five minutes, she went back and forth with someone on the other end, discussing Iris James. When she hung up, she looked at Six. "We have to go back to the conference room right now." She shuffled to her feet.

Six looked up at her with his fork in one hand and a mini mushroom in the other. "Can I finish my food first?" he asked her.

"You are finished," she said. "Now let's go."

Within the next twenty-four hours, the feds had Papa Bear's farm on round the clock surveillance. Phone taps and undercover agents pretending to be farmers with grown kids who had moved out in Harlem, Georgia; six miles away from the farm were deployed. They figured that if Iris James and Papa Bear were linked, this could be a major win for them. However, if they found Timbo's body out there, it would go down in United States history.

It was eight thirty a.m. when an undercover federal agent rode down a main road through Harlem Georgia in a UPS truck, and dressed in a brown UPS uniform. He was a young white guy who was actually born and raised in Valdosta Georgia and twenty-four years old. But there was a problem, Papa Bear's mailbox was on the main road and there were no trespassing signs all around his property, which was surrounded by four thin lines of barbed wire. The dense tree line wouldn't allow any by passers to see down to the house or the horse barn.

There was the dirt road that led to the house, but the feds knew that they didn't have any logical or legal reason to approach the house. They decided to bend the rules this morning. The UPS undercover turned the truck onto the dirt road. There were signs on both sides that clearly read, PRIVATE PROPERTY.

He drove further on, and spoke into a hidden microphone that looked like an expensive ink pen in his shirt pocket. "I'm now entering the dirt road. It's pretty bumpy and uneven, three feet high banks of dirt on both sides. Tall trees up ahead and a lot of thick bushes."

He drove further, the truck rocking side to side. The further he got, the thicker the sand got. Then he noticed two signs on each side: No Vehicles beyond This Point.

When he saw the signs, he pressed the brakes and stopped the truck. He put the pen up to his mouth. "I'm stopping here. There are two signs that say no vehicles beyond this point."

"Okay, don't go any further. Back up out of there." The person's voice was low and calm.

The driver put the truck in reverse, his eyes scanning around through the dense trees and bushes. Then he saw something move, it looked spooky, almost like a scene from the movie, *Children of the Corn.* A deer came out and stopped behind the truck, looking at him through the rearview. The driver pressed the brakes and jammed to a stop. He got out, left the truck running and walked around to the rear and stomped his foot to scare away the deer.

Chapter 16

At the all-white mansion in Miami, Pepé, Falisa, Amil, Papa Bear, Fly, Pig Man, Smurf and Iris all sat around inside the security room watching a projector screen that spread across the wall. On the screen, they were watching the white guy in the UPS truck running off the deer. Papa stood with his arms folded across his chest.

He looked at Amil who held the remote control, which was the size of a four by eight inch book. "Freeze his face, Amil."

Amil held the touch button pad in her lap. She looked down and touched a few buttons. She cropped his face, blew it up, and moved it across the screen.

Papa Bear moved over toward Falisa and Pepé, who was sitting next to each other on a suede love seat. "UPS don't come to the farm. If he's an agent, somebody tipped them." he was addressing them both.

Falisa looked up at him. "So what do you suggest, Papa?"

"Run his face and get a name. I think I need to be there."

Falisa's eyes nearly turned to slits as she stared up at him. "Slippers count. Did you clean up?"

"That's why I need to be there."

Pepé cleared his throat, and with his thick Colombian accent, he said, "I think we all should leave the country."

"I will agree with that for the family. But in my profession, I can't allow my actions to destroy what we have built."

"That's understandable." Falisa responded.

Amil then stood up holding the four by eight remote control like a school student would carry a book. She stood next to Papa Bear. "Bad idea, Papa."

"I agree with Amil." Falisa said with a smile, and then she stood up and eased her arm around Amil's neck. She kissed Amil's cheek and said, "Papa always thinks ahead. He's making the right decision."

Amil's face saddened. She turned toward Papa Bear, looked up into his eyes and he stared down into hers. They had an intense father daughter bond. Amil felt in her heart that something wasn't right. However, she knew how Papa Bear operated. He gave her a smile, leaned down, and pressed his forehead against hers. "Nothing can stop us," he whispered.

She wrapped her arms around his waist. Her head came to his chest and she laid it there for a moment. The rest of their family sat quietly. They all knew that if Amil and Falisa couldn't change Papa Bear's mind, then no one could. Moments later, Papa Bear went around the room, hugging each of them. They exchanged their goodbyes, and two hours later, Papa Bear was on interstate ninety-five, heading back to Georgia in a rental car.

Nearly thirteen hours later, Papa Bear pulled up on his property. It was after midnight, and the sky was dark. A light rain had fallen a couple of hours earlier and Papa was feeling the result of it as he drove down his uneven dirt road that led to his ranch home. He parked and got out, and stood next to the car as he scanned his property, much of it he couldn't see. But the surveillance equipment he had was some of the same equipment that the federal government used themselves. He shifted his head and body to the right. His eyes were on the horse stables that were nearly one hundred yards away, and illuminated by a halogen lamp post.

Papa Bear had cameras everywhere; sensor laser beams that could only be seen by the military or the feds. He turned around again, facing straight into the woods and stared blankly. Nothing seemed disturbed. He relaxed, shoved his left hand in his pocket and began walking toward the front door, removing a single key from his left pocket. He stopped, now he was having second thoughts, but that didn't stop him from pushing the key into the lock and twisting it. He turned the knob with the other hand and pushed the door open.

He stepped inside the dark front room, turned around, and looked out across his property. Papa Bear was very observant. He knew the feds were on to him. His gut feeling, nor his heart would allow him to think otherwise. Was he worried? Not at all. He closed the door, and then locked it. Next to him was an electronic numeric pad on the wall. There, he pressed a few numbers and a small light blinked green twice, and then it turned off.

He turned on the lights. His eyes swept across the room as he stood and listened to the stony silence. He walked through the house, moving light for a man his size. Papa Bear took off his steel toe boots before he crossed the threshold into the kitchen. When he stepped into his kitchen, he flipped on the light switch and looked around at the state-of-the-art appliances. The stove sat in the center of the kitchen on an island with off white marble tops where he cooked his famous meals for his family. Since he'd been plugged in with Falisa, he'd upgraded everything. Falisa had even convinced him to get a secret escape exit from the ranch home. Even though he did get it built, he didn't feel as if he would ever need to use it. However, tonight, he was going to test it out.

He thought about how tired he was from the road trip back from Miami. Papa Bear made himself a turkey and egg sandwich, showered and went to sleep.

When the sun came up a few hours later, there was a knock at his front door. Papa Bear's eyes opened. He grabbed the remote to his TV and pressed the power button and the screen went live. From the hidden surveillance camera on his front porch, he saw a couple standing at his door, a black couple who looked to be in their mid-forties. The lady held what looked like a cake box in her hand. The man was dressed in clean denim jeans, a Carhartt jacket, and worn down boots. The camera caught him from every angle.

Papa Bear sat up in bed. He slipped on a pair of clean socks and stepped into a pair of khaki pants, and then his boots, his eyes still on the TV, watching the couple on the front porch. Papa Bear stood, stretched his arms above his head, and silently yawned. As he walked down the hallway toward the living room, the house phone rang. He answered it while still heading toward the front door. It was Falisa on the other end, just as he was unlocking the door.

"It's not good, Papa." she said.

Papa Bear had the phone pressed to the side of his face as he stared at the unknown couple that stood before him. Then she went on, "It's not good at all."

"What is it?" he said into the phone. He flashed a smile at the couple, removed the phone from his face, and said, "Good Morning."

"The sour apple is still alive. It wouldn't surprise me if he was the one." She was talking about Six.

Papa Bear held his anger, and without another word, he ended the call and invited the undercover federal agents into the house.

Cole Hart

:

Chapter 17

Amil watched everything from the security room. On the big screen, she could see federal agents raiding Papa Bear's farm. They were coming from everywhere. Some wore fatigues and T-shirts, with vests, and masks covering the lower half of their faces. Some of them were in jeans and blue ATF jackets. Guns were drawn, and they were combing his property. Amil stared, sitting in the room all alone and filled with emotions to the point that she couldn't hold back her tears. Her heart felt so heavy; her lips began to tremble as well as her hands.

Then the screen went blank. Amil's eyes turned cold. She reached to her left, grabbed the remote, and pressed a couple of buttons. There was a shot of Papa Bear's kitchen, more federal agents stalking like trained assassins with their guns drawn. Amil stood up, walked to the wall, and pressed the intercom button for Falisa's room.

"Mother, can you come to the security room, please?"

"Is it Papa?"

Amil was wiping tears from her eyes, staring at the screen. That one went blank as well. Amil didn't respond, she slid down the wall and just shook her head from side to side. Pepé came through the door first and leaned down beside Amil. Before he could get a word out, Fly came in with Smurf behind him. The screen came back on. Papa Bear was laying in the middle of the living room floor.

Fly went to Amil, grabbed her hand, and pulled her up. He wrapped his arms around her; he couldn't afford for her to have a nervous breakdown. He took her out of the security room just as Iris and Falisa were approaching. They all met up in the hallway. Falisa and Iris looked directly at Amil. They'd both seen that look before, but Fly gave them a look and waved his hand dismissively. No words were exchanged. He walked off with Amil, holding hands like high school girlfriend and boyfriend.

Outside in the four-car garage, Fly's Lamborghini was parked. Next to it was a black on black Aston Martin four door. The keys were hanging inside a small box on the back wall. Fly looked at Amil. "Get in."

Amil looked at him, and then moved around to the passenger side of the Aston Martin. Fly unlocked the doors with the press of a button on the key chain. She opened the door, Fly opened his, and they climbed in at the same time. She closed her door and pulled her seat belt across her upper body.

Fly turned his head toward her. "Let's go somewhere. Matter of fact, I want you to take me shopping," he said soothingly.

Amil eased herself a little. There was still a stressful look in her eyes, but she managed a smile. "Where? It's eight in the morning, Fly."

The Throne 3

Fly eased the key into the ignition and started the Aston Martin. The engine purred to life and then it roared. "Well, we gonna ride around Miami and do some shopping." he said to her. Fly wanted to settle Amil, take her away to keep her mind off Papa Bear. He hated that she had to see it. That took something out of him, like a powerful blow to the stomach. She was still his little sister.

He reached up and pressed the button on the garage door opener that was clamped on his overhead visor. His eyes shifted to his rearview and he saw the door behind him inching its way up. He put the Aston Martin in reverse and backed out onto a smooth flattop of black asphalt that wrapped around the entire mansion. Fly looked at Amil as he slowly drove toward the front entrance.

When they got to the entrance, there was an eight-foot iron gate blocking it. A Colombian man, clean shaved and dressed in a suit was looking at Fly from behind the glass of the booth. He appeared into the doorway and Fly rolled his window down. "Do you want assistance, sir?" he asked Fly.

Fly nodded his head. The Colombian pressed a button and the gate rolled open. When Fly pulled the Aston Martian out onto the main street, a black Navigator pulled out in front of him and another one pulled behind him. On the inside of each Navigator were three hired Colombians from Pepé's cartel. All six men wore expensive suits and were armed with assault rifles. They were escorts.

A helicopter hovered above Papa Bear's farm, the spinning propellers ruffled the battered winter trees, and at some point, kicked up dust. Federal agents were combing the property inch by inch. They brought in forensic teams straight from Quantico to dust everything in the house. They wanted Iris James without a doubt, and they damn sure wanted to see if Timothy "Timbo" Walker's body was buried out here. They sat Papa Bear down on the sofa in his living room, his hands cuffed in front of him. Two hours had passed, and he hadn't parted his lips. Then, an agent came through the front door, his face pink and his eyes were blood shot red. He stared at Papa Bear, but he was talking to the other agents, looking at them from his peripheral vision.

"Oh, y'all can go ahead and book him."

"On what charges, sir?" One of the agents asked from the side.

"So far, we've dug up six graves. Six body bags. And the way it's looking, six murder charges." He smirked at Papa Bear as he delivered his words. He *knew* he had him.

Papa Bear took a deep breath, while he played the song, "Midnight Train to Georgia" in his head. Then he leaned back and closed his eyes. His head rested against the soft pillow of the sofa, and for the first time that Papa Bear could remember, he felt defeated.

Cole Hart

Chapter 18

Toronto, Canada

One year later

He no longer went by the name, Anthony "Six" Livingston. That was the old him. His new name was Gary Daniels, he was twenty-one years old, and he worked at The Royal Ontario Museum, which had more than six million items and forty galleries. Gary was still learning the entire museum. He started as a typical clean up guy, until after his first two months, and then he was a helper in the dinosaur gallery where he'd learned about the many different fossils.

One day, a few months back, one of the dinosaurs had accidently been knocked over. Gary made it his business to help the old Chinese man put it back together. From that point on, Gary Daniels was known throughout the museum as a hard worker. He assisted the tourists with items that they had heard about and couldn't find.

After Six had given the feds everything he knew, they'd allowed him, his mother, and elderly grandmother to go and live in Toronto, where they'd provided them with a four-bedroom home.

His mother and grandmother ran and operated their own soul food restaurant, called A Taste of Georgia, which had some of the best home-style cooked meals that Toronto had ever tasted.

Today, Six/Gary was at home with his Canadian girlfriend, Katrina, who he'd been with for the last eight months. They had a close relationship from the first day that they met at the food court in Toronto's Eaton Centre Mall at the food court. She had stepped to Six and told him that he looked like a rapper from Buffalo, New York. He ate it up. From there, they had lunch together, and then they went to the movies and on dinner dates. She took him to a Toronto Blue Jays game and he took her on tours of the museum.

Katrina sat next to him on the double stuffed sofa in their living room with her head in his lap while he played NBA live on the PlayStation. He put the game on pause and rubbed his fingers through her hair. She turned her head and looked up at him, her eyes were bright and innocent and her face was round with chocolate skin that was soft and pretty. Six adored her for several reasons. One, she was a college graduate and very independent. Katrina didn't have any kids and she worked as a real-estate broker and brought in a nice income.

Staring into her eyes, Six held her face between his hands, caressing her soft skin with his rough fingertips. He finally leaned down and kissed her lips. She smiled, closed her eyes, and kissed him passionately. Six lifted her up, stared in her eyes and kissed her again. She draped her arms around his neck. Between kisses, she whispered, "I love me some Gary Daniels."

He smiled, then said, "I love me some Katrina Daniels."

The Throne 3

She lit up like a tree on Christmas. "That's not my last name," she said in a joking manner.

"But I want you to have my last name," he said, and reached underneath the sofa pillow that was next to him and pulled out a black velvet ring box. He slid off the sofa onto one knee in front of Katrina. She gasped and covered her mouth with both hands. When he flipped the box open, there was a clean three-carat diamond sitting on a gold mount.

He looked into her eyes and asked her, "Will you marry me?"

She burst into tears and grabbed his face in her hands. She rained kisses all over his face as her tears flowed. "You know I will." she responded, her voice soft and low.

Six stood up, filled with emotions, desperately trying to push his old life away from his memory. He pulled her up, her head stopping just above his rib cage. They embraced. He rubbed his hand up and down the middle of her back, just as he heard a car pulling into the driveway. He turned and went to the window, parted the curtain and saw his mother's SUV pulling up.

Happily, he closed the curtain and went back across the room. He kissed Katrina on her lips. "It's my mama and granny. Let's surprise them."

Katrina grabbed both of his hands, held him tight because he was so anxious. When he heard the key in the lock, he looked in her eyes. "Wait until you see the expression on Mama's face. She loves you to death."

Katrina felt a wave of nervousness wash over her. "Let me go pee, don't tell them until I come back." She kissed his lips again, and then she turned and went toward the bathroom.

Gary's mother walked into the house first, with three Styrofoam trays of food stacked on top of each other inside a plastic grocery bag. She was dressed in black jeans, Nikes, and a T-shirt that had the words: A TASTE OF GEORGIA spelled across the front. He hugged his mother and kissed her cheek.

"Boy, what you so happy about?" she asked him. "Go get the bag from the backseat."

His grandmother came in behind his mother. She walked a little slower, slightly bent at the waist and wore a wig. He kissed her cheek on his way out the door. Walking outside, he yelled back. "Katrina is in the bathroom."

The outside was fresh, and the sky was bright. He got to the back door of his mother's Tahoe and opened it. There was a big, black trash bag on the floor with a knot tied into the top of it. Six frowned at the size of it. *What's in here?* He thought to himself. He knew his mother was connected to all types of people through churches and their restaurant. He gripped the bag, lifted it out of the Tahoe, and sat it on the ground.

When he closed the door, a white Honda Accord pulled up and stopped, as if the brakes had jammed abruptly. Six turned around and faced the street where the car was sitting. For some reason, he froze. He could see a silhouette from behind the light tint on the window. Before he could move, the window lowered, and the lady in the driver seat was holding pamphlet.

Cole Hart

She greeted him with a smile. "God bless you."

Six's heart fell into the pit of his stomach. He looked at the lady. She wore glasses and had an old-fashioned hairstyle. The first thing that came to mind was Jehovah Witness. *Damn!* He said to himself.

"Is your mother home?" the lady asked as she turned off the engine on the Honda Accord.

She opened the door. Gary noticed that the lady in the car craned her neck to look past him. He turned around and saw his grandmother, just as she was saying, "Ya'll come on in, baby."

Gary lifted the bag and heaved it over his right shoulder, thinking that this was definitely the wrong time for these damn Jehovah Witnesses. *Grandma stays fucking with these people,* he thought with annoyance. He shook his head as he was walking past his grandmother and into the house.

He turned around after he crossed the threshold. "You want the door closed, Grandma?"

Chapter 19

She turned around and faced him. Her eyes were low and tired, but she had a strong voice. "Get my bible off my night stand, for Grandma." Then she turned back around and faced the Jehovah Witness lady and the older man on the passenger side. They both stepped out of the white Honda Accord. The lady on the driver side wore a dark blue dress and some cheap looking flats. She carried her Bible, and her hands were full of pamphlets.

She closed her door and waited for the elderly gentleman to come around to her side. He walked with a cane and a noticeable limp. He was dressed in khaki pants, a brown blazer over a white button down shirt, and a fake pair of Rockports. He carried his bible as well, and wore a gray beard, a nappy salt and pepper afro, and a pair of wire-framed eyeglasses.

When he finally closed his door and came around to the driver side, Fly and Iris walked up the driveway and on to the front porch.

Six came back to the door and handed his mother her Bible. Fly looked at him briefly; he knew Six didn't recognize him. He watched him hand over the Bible and without a word, turn around and close the door. Fly extended his hand out to the lady and moved his mouth with a horrible sound. "Guuud bless." He said in a shaky voice.

She shook his hand and gave him a smile. "God bless you too, baby."

Inside the house, Six stood at the window, peeping through a small slit in the curtain. His grandmother was now sitting down in a rocking chair, and so were the two Jehovah Witnesses. When all three of them opened their Bibles, he closed the curtains and turned around to face Katrina and his mother. They were sitting on the sofa next to each other, examining the engagement ring. He laughed.

"For Grandma to be a Christian, she sho' be kickin' it wit' da' Jehovah Witness people a lot." He walked over and sat in the black leather recliner.

His mother looked up at him. "You leave yo' grandma alone."

"You can leave my grandmother alone." Katrina added with a smile. Her eyes sparkled with excitement.

Then, before he could respond, the front door opened and Six's grandmother peeped her head inside. "Baby, show him where the bathroom is." she said to Six.

Fly appeared at the door and limped his way into the living room. He paused, closed the door behind him, turned around and faced the room. Gary looked at Fly and noticed that he was wearing hearing aids in both of his ears. He almost laughed when he stood up, shaking his head at the silly old man. He just didn't like the aggravating Jehovah's Witnesses.

Fly bowed his head at the women, and they acknowledged him in return. "This way, sir." he said and led Fly down the hallway.

Fly walked slowly, while Gary was nearly ten feet ahead. Fly paused after he passed the rear of the sofa. Oblivious, Six continued moving forward. Without warning, Fly reached underneath his blazer, pulled out a specially made silenced .22 automatic, aimed it at the back of Katrina's head, and pulled the trigger. It sounded like someone sneezed. Her head went forward, and within the next two seconds, he hit the mother with a slug to the base of her skull. Two shots.

When Six turned around and looked at the person who he thought was an old man, he was facing death. "Go on inside, nigga," Fly whispered.

Six raised his hands. A look of panicked fear was in his eyes. He slowly turned and put his hands on the knob. "Man, please don't hurt my family."

"Nigga shut the fuck up and get inside. Yo' family already dead."

Fly aimed the gun at his mid-section and squeezed the trigger. Then, he lifted the cane and pushed Six with it until he went into the bathroom. Six's adrenaline began pumping as he stumbled backwards and kneeled defenseless on the floor. Fly walked in, closed the door, and stood over him. "Monkey ass nigga," Fly whispered. "You went against the grain."

Six couldn't respond. He didn't know what was going on. All he knew was that the feds were supposed to be protecting him. His eyes showed pain. "What you talkin' bout?" Six asked. The small hole in his shirt was framed by a circle of blood.

"Papa Bear told me to tell you to keep your hand pressed against the bullet wound, and you'll live longer. The twenty two bullet will travel through your body like cancer."

Papa Bear? He thought. He tried squinting his eyes to see if he recognized Fly. But Fly shot him in the left side of his stomach, and he yelled out in pain, like a wounded animal.

"Yeah, I'm Fly, nigga." Fly gritted his teeth and mumbled his words.

"I thought you were dead."

Fly laughed halfheartedly. "You took the words right out of my mouth." Then he quietly said, "I been up here in Canada a whole year, tryin' to catch you, baby boy. Eatin' at that damn nasty ass restaurant of yours." Fly shook his head from side to side in disgust. Silence hung in the air between the two of them.

Fly stared down to where he'd shot him. The blood was now seeping slowly through his fingers. Fly's eyes went back to his. "I won't sit around long and talk bad about you, Six. But I've shot and killed niggas for you and this the reward I get?" he took another deep breath, the gun dangling in his hand. Fly was beginning to sweat underneath his fake beard and wig, and Six was looking more drained by the minute. Then Fly said, "You wanna know what really hurt me about you the most?"

He didn't respond, his eyes were turning glossy and tears were running down his cheeks. He probably had another eight to ten minutes to live. Fly raised his gun up and aimed it at his left temple. "You allowed your treacherous behavior to get your mama and grandmamma murdered too." Fly pulled the trigger and Six's entire body jerked and then stopped moving. Fly stood there for a moment, and then he pressed his mid-section with the bottom of his cane to see if he was still alive.

The pressure that Fly applied made blood gush from the bullet holes in his stomach. Fly knew he was dead, but he shot him in the back of his head for security purposes. He tucked his gun underneath his jacket, reached his hand under his shirt and gripped the door handle with it. When he stepped out into the hallway, Iris was standing there waiting for him. She looked him up and down to see if he was all right. He was.

Beside her on the floor was a red gallon jug of gas. She picked it up. "Wait for me in the car."

Fly walked back toward the living room. He passed all three bodies without looking at them and headed out the door. Iris went into the bathroom and doused gasoline all over Six's body and the wood cabinets and walls. She backed herself out the bathroom and poured a trail of gas as she made her way into the living room. She circled the floor where the bodies were slumped over.

When she got to the door, she struck a match, dropped it on the floor, and watched the living room turn into flames.

Chapter 20

"Son of a bitch." The tall white federal district attorney said into the phone from the privacy of his own office. Sitting behind his high glossed mahogany desk, his face turned dark pink, and his eyes had turned to slits. Still holding the phone pressed against the side of his face, he couldn't believe what he had just been told. He'd just gotten word that their star witness was dead and that made their case against Papa Bear weak as a matchstick.

Sweat began trickling down the side of his face. He pulled out the top drawer to his left and retrieved an asthma pump. He pushed his chair out and stood up. "So what, we can still get him. What else we got on him?"

"Without the murder conspiracy and the Livingston guy, all we can get him with is cruelty to animals."

The district attorney, whose name was Ronald Tuff, could only think that his agent friend on the other line must've been talking out the side of his neck, he was confused himself, now. After a long deep breath, he said into the phone. "Wait a minute, maybe we're talking about two different cases. I'm talking about the old man in Harlem Georgia, goes by Papa Bear. Government name, Robert English, the six bodies that were found on his property.

"Listen Ronald, we're talking about the same case. The same person. All except for the six bodies. We thought you knew about that."

Ronald Tuff's eyebrows bunched together. "Knew about what?"

"The body bags. There were only five dogs buried in the body bags. Oh, and a horse that had been shot and wrapped in black plastic. Cruelty to animals is all we can charge him with. Other than that, he's clean."

Ronald Tuff tilted his head backwards and stared up at the ceiling, sweat was pouring harder now and he wiped his hand over his face. *This can't be,* he thought. *We don't make rookie mistakes like this.* He took another drawn out deep breath and walked around his desk, the phone still pressed against his face. The voice came from the other end.

"We'll still get a conviction."

Ronald Tuff looked even more disgusted now. He barked into the phone, "What? Fucking buried Pit-bull. That's nothing. He'll be out in two years. Damnit, if not before then. He's already done a year. I just can't believe it." He shook his head, picked up a pack of Marlboro cigarettes, removed one from the pack and fired it up.

He blew out a stream of smoke and stared out his office window. Then without another word, he politely hung up.

Cole Hart

The federal agent that was just on the phone with Ronald Tuff went by the name, George Alexander. He was a black man in his mid-forties and had been a special agent for almost twenty years. He sat behind his desk, staring at the phone and allowing the buzzing sound to rattle in his ear. He finally hung it up, feeling relieved and satisfied with the favor that he'd done for his longtime friend and associate, Pepé.

George Alexander was the Colombian's inside connect. It was he who knew about Six and his whereabouts, and he was paid handsomely for this reliable information. Now, George Alexander was ready for his bonus that Pepé and Falisa had promised him. He got up from his desk inside his office in downtown Miami and pulled an untraceable cell phone from his desk drawer. He turned it on and punched in Pepé on speed dial.

Pepé answered, pretending to be a manager at a restaurant. "Thanks for calling Chick-Fil-A. This is Jose, how may I help you?"

George grinned. He admired how Pepé always disguised himself when he answered the phone. "Good, business as usual." was all George Alexander said into the phone.

"Gracias, my friend. What would you like to eat?"

"A two piece chicken would be fine." He had just told Pepé that he wanted two million dollars wired into his private account.

"No problem, my friend. Twenty four hours." Then he hung up.

When George hung up his personal phone, he quickly collected his belongings, everything from family photos to air fresheners. Today would be his last day working as a federal agent. He had over twenty five million dollars spread around the world in several offshore accounts. After he got everything together that he wanted to leave with, he calmly left his office and took the elevator down to the parking deck and got into the front seat of his government issued blue sedan.

When he started the car and pulled the gear down into reverse, the entire car roared and exploded into flames. *KA-BOOM, KA-BOOM*, the car windows shattered into tiny pieces and George didn't know what hit him. But Pepé did. He wasn't trying to leave any paper trails, and nothing to link him or his family.

Chapter 21

Pepé and Falisa were watching CNN news together while eating lunch in the all-white mansion. On the TV, the news reporter was standing in front of the federal building downtown with the swat team. Several fire trucks and police cars were blazing with lights behind her. Pepé's eyes were staring into the TV, a fork in his right hand with a big piece of lobster tail meat on the end of it. He stuffed it into his mouth, chewed, and watched in silence. Pepé wanted to make sure that the bombing didn't hurt anyone else. So far, everything was looking good. He looked at Falisa who was watching the TV; an untouched salad was in front of her. She was wrapped in a terry cloth robe. Falisa picked up the remote, aimed it at the TV, and pressed a button.

The screen went blank and she faced Pepé with an unreadable stare. "I don't understand the purpose behind that," she said calmly. "I mean, wasn't he a valuable piece?"

Pepé chewed casually as he looked up at Falisa. "He *was* a valuable piece." He said, and then added, "After an agent retires, they're no good to us anymore."

Falisa sat quietly for a moment. She looked away from him, picked a small piece of chicken chunk from her salad, and tossed it in her mouth. She chewed it. Her eyes went back to Pepé. The look that he gave her was telling her he didn't care, and as the wife, she didn't care either.

She changed the subject. "Amil wants to go on a vacation. She wants you to approve it."

Pepé sat his fork down with a small shrug of the shoulder, "She don't need my approval," he said in his thick accent. "Where is she trying to go?"

"She wants you and me to take her to Chia, Colombia."

"That's not a good idea. It may be a war in the next month or so, and our Cartel may have to relocate."

"We should be able to go over there for a few days, at least."

"Sounds like you're anxious to go yourself."

Falisa smiled, her teeth were white and even like she was on a Crest commercial. "If this was a test, we would have the highest score in class. We got Papa Bear's situation, Fly and Iris took care of the rat, Smurf and Pig Man are handling all the street business. No paper trail for us. Let's take a vacation and let Amil see your country."

Pepé had to smile. He knew Amil just like everyone else did. And in the back of his mind, he knew Amil was up to something. "And when is Fly and Iris coming back?"

"They've already left Canada, but they went to New York on my call. All enemies must be crushed. Totally."

The Throne 3

"Understand." He leaned over toward Falisa and kissed her lips. "Chia it is, then."

Falisa slid down from the cushioned stool, wrapped her arms around Pepé's neck, and held on to him. His hand slipped inside her robe and he rubbed her breast and nipples. "Let's go to the bedroom." Falisa whispered.

Pepé picked Falisa up and carried her from the kitchen up the stairs and into the master bedroom. He carefully laid her down on the bed and opened her bathrobe, exposing her perfect breasts and flat stomach. Pepé kissed her stomach and drew an invisible line with his tongue down to her clit. Her stomach rising and falling, she spread her legs wider and her eyes went down. She loved the way he ate her, and the faces that he made was something that she enjoyed seeing. Pepé's mouth went to her clit and sucked on it slowly.

"Hmmm," she moaned. She felt herself getting wetter by the minute. She grabbed the back of his head and played in his curly hair. Pepé licked between her split and Falisa's eyes rolled to the back of her head. Her nipples got harder and her breathing was coming faster. Pepé worked himself out of his robe without moving his mouth and tongue away from Falisa's vagina. Falisa pulled on him, telling him with her eyes that she wanted him inside of her. Pepé began to make his way up her body, kissing her stomach and sucking on her nipples. To him, Falisa tasted like pure honey, it was still in his mouth. Obviously expensive, and he loved it.

He finally eased himself inside of Falisa and any problems he'd had before this very moment were gone. The feeling was

Cole Hart

112

heavenly. Pepé pumped and rotated his hips a couple of times and prayed that the new pill he'd taken before lunch would work. *So far, so good,* he said to himself. He smiled, put his mouth on hers and they kissed as he went deeper.

Falisa's mouth formed a perfect O, no words came out, but he knew he was handling business. Her nails clawed his back. He went deep again, and Falisa began moaning and loosening up a little. She knew he would've normally came by now, but he didn't and that was a good thing.

Falisa rotated her hips, meeting his long deep thrusts that were filling her up from every angle. "This your pussy, Daddy."

Pepé liked that. Her words had given him a surge of energy. He hooked his arms underneath Falisa's legs and locked her in. Then, Pepé slid in and out of her until she yelled and begged. Falisa loved it; she came twice, back to back. Pepé flipped her over on her hands and knees and fucked her for another hour, and then they went to sleep.

Around noon the next day, Falisa and Amil were standing in front of the mansion with nearly twenty pieces of luggage and duffle bags. Amil was growing up fast, and her body was now fully developed, looking like a younger Falisa with thick thighs, small waist and firm breasts. She was dressed in jeans, Air Max Nikes, and a halter-top. Falisa wore a jogging suit and Nikes; nothing spectacular, with LV shades on her face.

Their limousine crept from around the rear of the mansion. A Colombian was behind the wheel and another one was on the passenger side. When the limousine stopped, both of the

Colombians stepped out in black shoes, black slacks, and black
pullover shirts that were long sleeved. They greeted Falisa and
Amil both with a handshake and a nod of the head. They opened
the rear door and the trunk. One of them waited by the rear
passenger door while the ladies loaded in. The other Colombian
carefully loaded their luggage into the trunk.

Pepé kissed Amil on her cheek when she slid into the rear of
the limousine, then he kissed his wife. He was dressed in a
cashmere sweat suit, a thick link around his neck. His hair was
slicked down and brushed to the back. He looked through the
tinted window, the driver was now closing the trunk, and his
bodyguards both loaded into the front.

When the dark panel inched half way down, the Colombian
said to Pepé in Spanish, "Air strip?"

"Si," was all Pepé said.

The panel went back up and Pepé clapped his thick hands
together and rubbed them. "Colombia, here we come."

Amil smiled at Pepé, and then said, "I want to see it."

And she surely would.

Chapter 22

There was nothing 'spur of the moment' about Fly and Iris' decision to go to Long Island, New York. It was a plan that they'd come up with while they were still tracking Six in Canada. And now Fly was back on Hawk's trail again. He wasn't going to rest until he put Hawk in a casket. However, he would be sure to handle business this time. In the Hamptons, Fly and Iris were renting out a luxurious five-bedroom home for eleven thousand a week. It was paid in advance for four months. Even though the money wasn't an issue, they had every reason to pay the price, because they'd gotten an official address on Hawk from Pepé, by way of the late George Alexander.

On this particular morning, Fly and Iris were lounging around the house in expensive sleepwear inside the billiards room. Fly stood at one end of the table, chalking up his pool cue. He looked at Iris standing at the other end. She was leaning over, both hands pressed against the rail of the table.

With a small smile, her eyes cut up at him. "You don't shoot pool, Fly." She shook her head, smiling at him because he was acting like he was a real professional billiards player.

"You just rack the balls," he said.

Iris came from her end of the table in long confident strides, walked right up to him, reached inside his robe, grabbed his dick, and began caressing his balls. Then she kissed him.

Between kisses, Fly said, "I'm talkin' 'bout the balls on the table."

They both laughed as she wrapped her arms around Fly and stared him dead in his eyes. Fly leaned his pool cue against the side of the table, then both of his arms slipped inside her robe and he cupped her nicely rounded ass.

"Sometimes I be feeling so guilty." Iris said. Her voice was low and soft.

Fly pulled her closer. He was strong and she felt the power. "What I told you about that?" he said confidently. "We the team."

He eased his tongue inside her mouth and she relaxed and closed her eyes. Then he whispered in a joking manner, "Long as you don't run off with a nigga who got both of his legs."

She playfully punched him in his chest. "Stop playing with me, Fly. I'll never leave you, not even if my life depended on it." She snuggled up close against his neck, breathing lightly on his skin. Fly then whispered softly, "We get this nigga, Hawk. We gon' retire."

"That sounds wonderful." Then she paused. Silence hung in the air. "I'll go ahead and tell you this now, because it's very important," she whispered.

Fly squinted a little, and a small wave of nervousness washed over him. He pulled back from her and looked her dead in her eyes. "I'm listening."

"I'm pregnant, but I'll have an abortion for the sake of us and our line of work."

Fly was devastated. He couldn't believe what he was hearing. *Pregnant? Abortion? Damn! What the fuck am I supposed to do?* His eyes began darting from side to side. He was actually trying to see if she was joking. Since they'd been together nearly every day for the past year, Fly had found her to be somewhat a comedian. But not today, this was real, and it was written all over her face.

"Well, you already know what that means."

Fear jumped into Iris' eyes. She realized it and tried to get herself together. Her mouth and throat turned dry, then she said, "No, what?"

"You get to go back to the mansion in Miami, unless you wanna go to Atlanta with January?"

The questions sat between the two of them for what seemed like forever, their eyes staring into each other's. Her heart beat erratically, her mind raced. *I shouldn't have told him,* she thought. She took a deep breath. "I'm staying. I don't have no other choice."

"Yes you do. You got a grandchild for my mama."

"I'm three weeks. If we don't have him in three weeks, I'll leave."

Cole Hart

The Throne 3

Now Fly was quiet, his eyes on her hard. He reached and grabbed both of her hands and held them in his. Fly looked her square in the eyes. "After three weeks, whatever the situation is, we leaving." Then he hugged her and kissed her cheek. In his mind, he knew their vacation time in the Hamptons had just gotten shorter.

The following morning, Iris was dressed in black spandex pants and a top. She wore AM FM headphones and ankle weights. She was speed walking in the fog with a blond white girl who was staying in one of the huge estates. Iris didn't get her name, and she didn't give one either. They were both speed walking in the same direction. Iris was swinging her arms, moving quickly. She had Hawk's estate address tattooed on her brain. Every house up there was hung, and the majority of them were sitting off on its own private property. She saw her street where she had to turn off at, and tapped the white girl on the arm to let her know that she was departing. They smiled and waved each other off.

Iris made a right, her pink and gray Nike sneakers moving across the newly paved asphalt. She passed by the first mansion on her left, which sat back from the street about forty yards. It was three stories and bricked up with a stone front facing and a lot of glass. The street was winding and going uphill and her legs were chopping like scissors, her arms bent upwards and the left one was in sequence with her right leg and vice versa. She passed private gated estate after estate, on either side of the street. An all-white old model Jaguar came creeping towards her with their high beam fog lights on. She didn't even turn her head towards it, but she caught a glimpse of the driver from her peripheral vision and noticed that it was an older white man behind the wheel. Iris made her face turn up into a smile then turned it off like a light switch. She was cautious and very careful this morning. Walking through one of the most exclusive and richest neighborhoods in the United States was something that she knew she couldn't play any games with.

As she moved up the winding street, it began to straighten out. She looked to her left. There was wide spacious green lawn underneath the thinning layer of fog. A beautiful three-story mansion with an all glass front, outlined with stones, sat at least two hundred yards away from the street. *Damn!* Iris said to herself. *This shit is nice.* She continued her same pace, never breaking stride. Another automobile was coming her way. This time it was a plain Buick with four doors, the high beams on. Iris gave another smile as the car passed.

She walked across the street to the side where the estate was sitting. She slowed her pace as she approached the opening of the newly paved driveway. There wasn't a security gate or guard booth. She stopped, bent over and put her hands on her knees, pretending to be tired.

Then, without warning, she turned and walked straight up the driveway and headed towards the huge seven-bedroom estate.

Chapter 23

The closer Iris got to the front of the mansion, the more impressed she became. The air was turning damp and blanketed with a very light misty drizzle. Only thirty yards away, she could see a pair of bone-white doors that were at least ten feet wide and twelve feet high. They were definitely hand crafted, designed with twin brass lion heads, which frowned at her. Scanning the grounds, she didn't see a car, but there was a four-bay garage sitting around the side. In Iris' mind, she knew she had to play her position, which consisted of pretending to be a resident in the neighborhood. *It's so quiet and peaceful out here,* she thought as she climbed the four steps that were in the shape of a half circle.

Here we go. She said to herself and pressed the illuminated doorbell. She heard it chime on the inside, then she waited. Five seconds... Ten seconds... Thirty seconds... One minute passed. She pressed the button again; she heard it chime for the second time. Five seconds... Ten seconds. Then she heard the locks being released from the inside. The door on the right side of her came open. Iris smiled at a dark skinned man that was very mean looking. He stood five-ten and was dressed in all black with a noticeable shoulder holster holding a fifteen round 9mm Smith & Wesson pistol. His eyes were beady and he looked Iris up and down while she did the same thing.

"Who are you?" The man asked her. He noticed her shapely body and was instantly impressed. He stared at her print between her legs.

Iris smiled. "Well actually, I was under the impression that Garth Brooks lived here. I'm Jasmine and I'm new to the neighborhood, I'm really sorry, sir." She started to turn and leave.

"Jasmine." he said. "That name fits you."

She turned around and faced him. Her smile was charming. Their briefly held each other. "Thank you," she said in her sexiest voice.

"Garth Brooks fan, ha?"

Iris shrugged. "I just thought I could get an autograph or something."

"So who are you with out here?"

Iris became curious, as if she didn't understand his line of questioning. She looked at him more closely. "I don't understand."

"You are with who?"

"Actually, I'm visiting. My mother's husband just moved out here. My family owns oil wells and tankers. We're from Nottingham, Pennsylvania."

His eyes were on her even harder, but he turned on his charm and gave her his hand to shake. She took it and held his hand.

"And you?" Iris asked him. She turned on her seductive stare.

Cole Hart

"This is the estate of Timothy Walker Jr., I'm the housekeeper."

Her gaze went down to his gun then back up into his eyes. "A housekeeper with a gun! I think that's sexy."

"I tell you what, why don't you come in for a minute."

"I'm in the middle of working out." She said in a low, sexy tone. Then she added, "I don't really wanna meet anyone and I'm sweating and stuff."

"No one else is here. You don't have to worry about meeting anyone except me."

Iris gave a look as if it was a tough decision to make, then she said, "A few minutes wouldn't hurt."

"Excellent decision." He held onto her hand and carefully pulled her inside the marbled foyer. The housekeeper turned around to close the door and with swiftness, Iris removed his gun from his holster and aimed it directly at him. "Go ahead and lock the door."

He turned and faced her, giving her a cunning grin and slowly shaking his head. He locked the door, and when he turned back around, she sprayed him in the face with an odorless poison that took him down to his knees and made him bleed from his nose and mouth. Iris then slipped a pair of pantyhose over her face and tucked the gun under her arm.

She walked down into the living room. It was wide and spacious, with high ceilings, and very interesting. There were huge, expensive paintings hanging on every wall. She found a cordless phone sitting next to a suede loveseat. She picked it up, punched in Fly's untraceable number, and told him she was in.

Ten minutes later, Fly was there. Dressed in a Dickie overall, he stepped down from the passenger side of a service van with no rear windows and a pool cleaning company logo plastered on both sides. The driver was a quiet black man in his late forties, who was familiar with the New York scene. Another associate of Papa Bear's. The rear van door popped open and two older gentlemen stepped out. All four of them were dressed identically in Dickie overalls.

Fly carried a small backpack across his left shoulder, and one of the two men in the rear came out with a waterproof duffel that was nearly four feet long. Fly led the way up the stairs, and the other two gentlemen followed behind him. The door was already ajar when they got to it. Fly walked through the door first, one of the older men behind him stopped at the door and carefully wiped everything down, including the brass handles, the lion heads, and the button for the doorbell, and then he walked inside and pulled the door closed with a handkerchief.

Inside the foyer, the lifeless housekeeper was still lying on the floor, blood seeping from his nose, mouth and even his eyes and ears. He stopped there, kneeled down next to him and checked his pulse in his neck and wrist. He was clearly over with like the end of a movie. And he was going to clean him up and make him disappear.

Fly found Iris standing in the middle of the living room floor, staring up at the huge life sized painting. Fly stood next to her. He was now looking up as well. The huge oil painting was a beautiful piece of Timbo standing up, dressed in a three-piece pinstripe suit, holding an old school Tommy Gun. The picture was detailed to perfection. Timbo was holding a chain in his other hand that was wrapped around the neck of a black panther. The cat had live bright eyes and Timbo was looking serious, and very intimidating.

Fly studied the painting, detail for detail. Now he was thinking harder about Hawk. Fly turned around, faced the other wall. There was a painting of Hawk and Timbo standing next to each other, both of them dressed identically in cocaine white suits with red shirts underneath. A gold plate beneath the photo read: Like Father- Like Son.

Fly nodded his head slowly. He and Iris walked through the huge estate, staring at picture after picture. There were paintings from Pablo Picasso and other art from Andy Warhol. But what really caught Fly's attention was a classic painting, just like The Last Supper, but Timbo was in Jesus' place, sitting at the head of a long table in yet another suit, a plate full of money was in front of him. Hawk was next to him with his own plate full of money in front of him. Fly scanned the picture and recognized Cory's face, and then Ox's face, Lex was there too. Two females, and a couple more faces completed the portrait. Everyone had had a plate full of money before them. Fly covered his mouth and studied the painting. He wondered how much he'd paid for it.

He looked at the old man. "Take that down." Fly told him.

Now he would wait.

Chapter 24

Down in Miami at the all-white mansion, Hawk stood in the middle of Falisa's living room floor with two of his associates, staring around as if he was caught up in a maze. Dressed in a black silk button up shirt, black slacks and cocaine white alligator skin shoes, his gun was in his hand. A female and another guy came to the rail at the top of the stairs. The guy looked down at Hawk and said, "This muthafucka is empty."

"You mean to tell me ain't nobody here?" Hawk said, sounding very disappointed. He tucked his gun in his waist and then put his hands in his pockets. Hawk began walking through the mansion. He yelled back up the stairs, "Check the security system. Find any video tapes and cameras. Look for any hidden surveillance equipment."

Hawk paused in front of the huge fireplace. There was a painting of Falisa sitting on her throne, her right leg crossed over her left. Hawk smiled, because of the way Fly was looking standing next to his mother. Amil was on the other side of the chair. *She's grown up into a young lady,* Hawk thought. He nodded and shifted his eyes back to Fly. He was dressed in a double-breasted white suit with gold buttons. Standing firm with a white and gold cane in front of him, his eyes were cold and still.

The Throne 3

"You died and left your mother and sister in this world all alone… with me." He spoke to the painting as he shook his head in disgust.

He walked up closer to the mantelpiece just underneath the painting and grabbed the marble and gold urn with the cremated ashes of Ox, which was supposed to be Fly. Hawk had been closely following Fly's murder case all the way down to the guilty plea, and until they pronounced him dead in his cell on Rice Street. He took the urn and sat down on the sofa. He removed the top and looked inside. The ashes were off white in color, with grey and black pebbles scattered throughout. He tilted it; feeling a bit unsatisfied because didn't get a chance to kill him.

On the glass coffee table in front of him, he dumped the ashes on the table, scattered them with no remorse whatsoever. Then he tossed the urn to the side. It shattered into tiny pieces and scattered across the marble floor. He turned his eyes up to his female companion who stood in the middle of the floor, watching him.

"Well, the lil nigga dead." He shrugged his shoulders and sounded as if he didn't care about him at all. And he didn't. "What you think our chances are of his mother and sister coming back in the next day or so?"

The girl stepped closer toward Hawk, anxious to respond to his statement. "My opinion, we should comb the entire estate first. I'm sure we can find something."

"I just want to kill them and leave." He scooted back on the sofa, removed his gun and sat it next to him. He crossed his legs and spread his arms out across the back of the sofa. He rubbed his hand across the material. *Damn! This sofa has nice material,* he thought. *Very expensive taste.* He stood up quickly. "Matter of fact, I think I can fuck the mother. She liked Timbo, I'm sure she'd like me."

"You a Don, baby. Damn right she's gonna like you," the girl said with confidence.

Hawk looked up when he saw his other male associate come back to the rail upstairs. A satisfied grin was on his face. He looked down at Hawk. "All security systems have been shut down. They had some real fancy shit, too."

"And everything is clear?" Hawk asked.

The guy's face turned serious, and then he folded his arm across his chest. "That's my word."

Hawk was instantly satisfied, he knew if his associate put his word on it, it was etched in stone. And that was that. Hawk looked at the girl. "Let's take a tour. See what's going on in this mansion."

Three days had passed, and Hawk still hadn't showed up at his own estate. Fly was getting restless. He'd called and ordered ten men to come to New York and wait at his rental house. Five were there with him and Iris, and five were at Hawk's place waiting. He was on the outside kitchen deck laying back in a recliner beach chair. Iris was next to him, reclined as well. She was sipping orange juice from a straw. Iris was dressed a colorful sundress, her nails painted and her eyes hidden behind a pair of Versace sunglasses. A small table separated them. On it was a cordless phone sitting inside the charger, a pitcher of ice with two bottles of spring water, and one small can of V8.

Fly sat up, dressed in simple linen pants, boat shoes by Polo and a thousand dollar Dolce & Gabbana hand painted T-shirt. He opened the V8, turned it up, and nearly drank the whole can.

The cordless phone rang. When she saw that he wasn't going to answer it, Iris reached and grabbed it, but was too late. The caller had hung up. Iris looked at and her eyes went to Fly in question. They knew that the only people with this number were the immediate family, Falisa, Amil, and Smurf. Not even Pig Man knew it. Iris held it clutched in her hand. She sat up and was easing her feet into her sandals, when the phone rang again.

"Hello." Iris said after pressing the ON button.

"Hey… This Smurf."

"Hey."

"Let me speak with him." Smurf said. He knew the phone was safe, but he still didn't want to call out Fly's name over the phone. Iris gave a look as if she could sense that something was wrong. Too much energy was in his voice.

She finally gave Fly the phone and he accepted it. "Yeah."

"Brah, your mama just called. We got a bad connection and I could barely hear her. She said she just tried calling you. Anyway, this the business. She said they have a minor problem."

Fly eyes turned cold and deadly. "I'm listening."

"We need to go to Miami first. She said she'll let us know the rest when we get there."

Fly held the phone to his face. Something was wrong. He could feel it running through his veins. Then he said into the phone. "What you think?"

"It's something to do with that nigga, Hawk. She said his name, but like I said, we need to go to Miami.

Chapter 25

Fly and Iris flew to Miami in the comfort of the family jet, in total silence. Fly had the small TV on that was built inside the wall. He wasn't watching it, though. Something was on his mind, he was trying to maintain, trying to keep his game face on to keep from displaying his anger. Their personal stewardess for the G4 came out with a cart, and on the cart were two stainless steel trays.

With a smile, she removed the stainless steel lids and handed Fly a plate full of fried shrimp that was lined up neatly around the plate. Fly took the plate and gave her a slight nod to show his thanks. She returned the same nod, removed the next top and turned to Iris who was sitting across from him. She received her plate, which was baked fish and asparagus, no starch and no bread for her. She stared at Fly, watching him with sharp eyes. He was young and smart, and very experienced in every way. She saw him lift the curtain and look out the window for at least twenty seconds, and then he shifted his head towards her.

"We in the bottom," was all he said. Another phrase from Miami.

Iris didn't respond. She used her fork and cut into the hot piece of fish, then casually eased it into her mouth.

They could feel the tires easing out. They would be landing shortly. They sat in silence for another twelve minutes or so, and then they landed onto the private airstrip and rolled down the runway until the jet came to a complete halt. It was dark outside. Fly hadn't moved, still staring out the window. He was worried to death about his family. He stood up with his cane, but he didn't move without Iris getting up first. When she did, he touched the small of her back and guided her towards the air stairs. He climbed down behind her.

There was a waiting limousine with the rear door open. Smurf was standing next to it with a cell phone pressed against the side of his face. He hugged Iris, and then she climbed inside the limousine. When Fly approached him, he handed him the phone that he was talking on. Smurf moved his mouth silently. "It's Falisa."

Fly took the phone. "Hello." he said in a low deep drawl.

"Hey." she said. There was static in the phone, but he could hear her. "Can you hear me?"

Fly's eyebrows bunched together. "I hear you." His eyes went to Smurf, who was standing there watching him.

".... At the mansion." Was all he heard from the other end.

"At the mansion, what?"

Falisa didn't respond, and now all he heard was clicking from her end. Fly was becoming agitated. He pulled the phone down from his face and said to Smurf, "Let's go to the mansion."

Smurf got in and slid across. Fly got in behind him and closed the door. Fly looked at Iris while still holding the phone pressed against the side of his face. The limousine began rolling. Fly said into the phone, "Can you hear me?"

Now the only thing he could hear was static, then the phone got quiet. Fly assumed the call had dropped. He had a frustrated look on his face. They rode in silence for the next twenty minutes. When they pulled up in the driveway of the all-white mansion, there were three black Hummers parked out front, nearly fifteen Colombians stood around in the dark. Some were armed, and others looked as if they were happy about something. Fly noticed this immediately.

A young Colombian greeted him when he stepped out. This was Pepé's nephew and he'd been in the United States for the last year and spoke very good English. He gave Fly his hand. Fly shook his hand and they exchanged a small embrace.

The Colombian whispered in his ear. "We got real good news." He pulled back, looking at Fly like a longtime friend. His name was Carlos, the son of Pepé's younger brother, Carlos. He was nineteen, a trained killer and millionaire himself. This was his first time meeting Fly.

Fly braced himself on his cane and worked his shoulders, standing fully erect at six feet tall with his thin, chiseled frame. He stared Carlos square in his eyes. "I'm listening." His tone of voice was easy, but his stomach was tight and the tingly feeling was running through his veins.

Carlos turned slightly to his left, touched Fly politely on his upper back. "Come with me." he said. Then he yelled out in Spanish to the remainder of his smaller and personal Cartel members, "Hey my friends, this is my uncle's stepson. He's the leader. Come."

Fly didn't know what he just said; all he knew is that all of the Colombians were falling into line directly in front of him. Smurf got out, and so did Iris. They were both armed and unaware of what was going on. When they saw the Colombians greeting Fly one at a time with strong handshakes and hugs, they quickly put away their guns and walked up behind Fly and Carlos.

Three minutes, and the greeting was over. Carlos led Fly, Smurf and Iris to the rear of one of the Hummers. He opened the back door. There were two body bags there, one on the floor and the other on the backseat. Carlos unzipped the one on the floor, there was a lifeless body of a dark skinned female. Her eyes wide open, staring into space.

"I don't know her," he said.

Smurf and Iris moved up and looked at the girl's face as well. Neither of them recognized her either. Fly looked at Carlos. Carlos unzipped the other plastic body bag, and there was a dead man laying the same way, his mouth slightly opened and his eyes were looking dead at Fly. Fly studied him, and he knew it wasn't Hawk.

He looked away from the body and put his eyes on Carlos. "Don't know him either."

The Throne 3

Carlos nodded, turned around and walked toward the rear of the mansion. Fly followed him, his cane tapping against the asphalt every time he put it down. Iris and Smurf walked with him. Carlos wasn't saying anything, but he moved with confidence, as if he knew there was a prize waiting. Fly was feeling more at ease now. When they got to the rear of the mansion, they climbed the wooden steps underneath the yard spotlights and moved onto the open deck. Carlos slid open the patio door and walked inside. Everyone was walking quietly behind him.

They walked through the spacious kitchen and into one of the carpeted hallways toward the west wing of the mansion. The group continued on to the cellar and the underground gallery.

They came to the entrance of the wine cellar, but it was blocked off by a huge and thick iron gate. To Fly's surprise; Hawk was standing just on the other side of it, trapped in the wine cellar. His eyes went to Fly and he studied him. Hawk had his hand wrapped around the neck of a thirteen hundred dollar bottle of Chateau-Paulet Cognac.

"Well, well, well…" Fly said as he walked up to the iron gate. His cold eyes were turning into pure happiness. He could never forget this face. "Baby Timbo."

Chapter 26

Hawk was sitting down on a crate; he looked tired and half-drunk. He turned up the bottle and brought it down. "Ain't nothin' baby about me, God," he nearly shouted.

Fly laughed halfheartedly. Then he asked him, "What brings you down to Miami?"

"Cut it out with the dumb ass questions." Hawk said, then added, "No beggin'. No pleading. Just do what you do."

"Nawl nigga, you owe me." Fly said and stepped back from the gate. He inched up his pants leg and showed Hawk his missing leg.

Hawk looked down at his leg. There weren't any emotions stirring in him because of it. He moved his eyes back up to Fly's eyes, and then he said, "Niggas lose limbs in the street every day. Just shows me how much of a soldier you were."

Fly let loose his pants leg and he stood up fully erect, balanced his cane in front of him, his right hand on top of his left. Iris and Smurf stood to his right in silence and Carlos to his left. Everyone knew this was a special moment for Fly, a day he'd been waiting on for years. Now he had him face to face, separated by an iron fence and security system that his younger sister had set for him.

Fly took a long deep breath and shook his head. Then he blurted out, "I took yo' Last Supper painting with you and Timbo and the rest of them dead ma' fuckas on the picture."

Hawk stared at him with a questioning and puzzled look on his face. His hand gripped tighter around the neck of the bottle, then he stood and walked up to the gate. "You got me in here like I'm some type of monkey on display."

"You did this to yourself, brother."

"We ain't brothers, God." Hawk said. His eyes turned cold; he was more frustrated than anything.

Fly looked around at Iris and Smurf. "Can somebody get me a chair?" he asked.

Smurf walked off and came right back with a chair on wheels. Standing behind it, he pulled up behind Fly and held the chair steady as he sat down. Smurf reached around for Fly's cane. He wanted him as comfortable as possible for this. Hawk was a prized catch for this family, and everyone in it has felt pain from his wrath. Even Smurf nearly died behind Hawk's actions.

Fly cleared his throat and got comfortable in his chair. Before he got started with Hawk, he looked up at Carlos. "Tell your people to get the boats ready. We going out to the water."

Carlos' face was unreadable. "The yacht?"

"Naw, we gon' need the air boats tonight. Go ahead and take them other two bodies out to the Everglades. Feed 'em to the gators." Fly turned away from Carlos and looked at Hawk. He folded his arms across his chest. "Now back to you," he said. "You kidnapped my little sister." He counted that statement with his pinky finger. "By the order of Timbo." Fly gave a look as if he'd totally forgotten to say something. "Speaking of Timbo... yo daddy, not mine, because we're not brothers." He flipped his head up and back at Smurf. Then he looked at Hawk and pointed towards Smurf. "This is my brother, Smurf. He's a real brother. Matter of fact, he's so much of a brother, he killed yo' daddy, Timbo, on behalf of my sister and myself."

Fly paused, watching Hawk's eyes. The area was quiet and Hawk could only imagine the scene of how they'd killed his father. Hawk looked at Smurf and saw an evil aura glowing all around him. Smurf wasn't an angry looking guy, and he definitely wasn't much of a talker unless it was family and friends. And he wasn't about to start talking now, he was simply thinking, *let's kill him and move on.* However, he knew Fly like the back of his hand.

"He begged for his life, like a bitch. The same way you gonna beg for yours." Fly growled with pure animosity in his voice.

Carlos' deep voice was coming back down the corridor. He was on the phone, speaking to someone in Spanish. Everybody turned around and faced him. He was speaking fast and anxiously. Just as he was about to hand Fly the phone, the line disconnected again. The buzzing tone was in his ear and frustration was on his face.

Cole Hart

He leaned down and whispered to Fly. "In Chia and Bogotá, our families are under attack. Our family is safe. We have a bombproof mansion bunker underground. Your mother and sister are well taken care of. My uncle and father said there's nothing to worry about, and they'll call back over the weekend. And the message that your mother sent, is for you to go ahead and kill him."

Fly reached for his cane, thinking about what Carlos had just said. Something wasn't registering correctly. Smurf gave him his cane and he stood up. Fly pulled Carlos away from earshot of Hawk. "What you mean under attack?" His eyebrows bunched together.

"No worry." Carlos said and put his hand on Fly shoulder and looked him in his eyes.

"Call back." Fly demanded.

Carlos dialed the number. The phone rang twice and then it got quiet. He hung up and called again, this time no sound. He looked at Fly and pressed his lips together. Then he dialed the number again. It rang.

"Si." Pepé's voice came from the other end.

"Uncle Pepé." Carlos said, his eyes staring into Fly's with pure excitement.

"Falisa, please."

The line got quiet and Carlos was hoping it didn't disconnect again. Then Falisa's voice came through crystal clear. "Hello."

Carlos gave Fly the phone. "Hello." Fly said. "What's the problem over there?"

"Calm down, baby. Everything is good. We just can't leave right now."

Fly eased a little, he took a breath. "Where's Amil?"

"In the swimming pool. I'm looking at her right now. Trust me baby, we alright."

"Okay. I feel a lil better now. So, maybe a week or so?"

"A month at the most, but we're guaranteed safe as money in a bank vault."

Fly smiled. "That's all I needed to hear. Now let me go ahead and handle this business."

"That's right. I'll tell Amil I spoke with you. And we love you."

"Love ya'll too." Fly hung up and handed Carlos back the phone.

Chapter 27

Just over an hour later, the Colombians had Hawk tied, taped, and sitting in the backseat of one of the black Hummers. His hands were bound tightly in the front of him. The duct tape was so tight it felt like it was stopping his blood circulation. His ankles were bound tightly the same way.

Fly was in the rear of the Hummer with him, along with Smurf and Carlos. Iris stayed back at the mansion. He had other plans for her, he was definitely about to retire her. Fly was staring at Hawk, no smiling, no talking. No fear at all. *Nigga, you a dead man, tonight.* He thought to himself while watching him. Fly saw the features in his face that reminded him so much of Timbo, and that made matters even worse because he hated to be reminded of Timbo.

The one exception was the time Papa Bear dug Timbo up, cleaned the grave, put the dead horse in Timbo's place, and got rid of Timbo's body. Falisa thought that with his body being buried on the property, a dark cloud and evil spirit would be over the farm. That was after she'd been thrown from her horse. So with Papa Bear taking her advice, he'd removed all the other bodies that he'd had buried on his property as well, and put dead pit bulls in the shallow graves.

Fly smiled, thinking back. He turned his head to Smurf and lightly tapped him on his arm. "Tell this nigga that the Colombians chopped off my leg with an ax all because of his treachery."

Smurf moved his dreads away from his eyes and gave Hawk a cold and devious stare. "When you killed the old Colombian lady and her son down in Miami, we were blamed for it." he paused. "They chopped of my brother's leg with an ax. Then we were in prison for forty months, all the way in Chia, Colombia."

Carlos pulled out a cigar, closed his eyes, eased it underneath his nose and took in the aroma. He was staring harder at Hawk now, but he wouldn't say anything; this was Fly's moment of fame. Carlos lit his cigar, and the first stream of smoke he blew went straight into Hawk's face.

He frowned and turned his head away.

Fly watched him, imagining to himself how they were going to go out into the dark Everglades at two in the morning and feed him to the vicious alligators. He said to Hawk, "You fucked my sister up, mentally." Fly didn't have a cigar, but he reached for the one Carlos had and pulled it one time. He exhaled the smoke and gave it back, and then he touched his chest. "That hurt me to my heart."

"Just shows you how weak and emotional you are," Hawk said.

The left side rear door opened from the outside. An angry looking Colombian was standing there in a black fatigue top and pants. "We got the green light at the Everglades. Our people are waiting on us," he said in Spanish.

"Si." was all Carlos said.

The Colombian slammed the door shut. Carlos looked over at Fly and Smurf, the cigar still burning slowly. "Everyone is in place."

Fly nodded.

Smurf nodded.

The engine of the Hummer came to life. They could feel the vibrating of it through the seats. Fly looked to Hawk again, his armpits were soaked and his eyes were down toward the floor. He was lost in space, and now the only sounds that could be heard was the engine pulling. Everyone jerked a little, and the three Hummers pulled out of the driveway.

Fly's hatred was growing by the minute. "We still got the video tape you sent. Both of them." He paused, and then he clapped his hands one loud time and slowly rubbed his palms together. "Seriously, this is not a Spike Lee joint." Fly said to Hawk. "Those were some serious words."

Hawk raised his head and eyes all together. "What you did with Ox?" he asked stubbornly.

Fly's face turned into a smile. The Hummer picked up speed. "I wanted to kill him, but I didn't."

"So he's still alive?" Hawk asked.

Then Smurf spoke up. "Hell nawl nigga, we changed his face, made him look like Fly, and then we sent his ass inside the county jail to take my nigga's place. Then we killed him." Smurf smiled. "The same way we killed ya' potna' Cory in New York and his mama, same way we killed ya' daddy and ya' grandma and granddaddy. Same way we gon' kill you. After tonight, we'll probably throw a party to celebrate the glory of your demise."

Hawk looked at Smurf; venom was blazing from his eyes. They darted to Fly and Carlos and then to Smurf again. Hawk didn't think he would ever be caught up in a situation like this. Not the way he thought, anyway. He was always two or three steps ahead. He had millions spread out there somewhere. He wondered if they would let him make a phone call. *Just one is all I need.* He said to himself. Then he closed his eyes and rested his head against the leather.

They continued on, riding in silence. They were on interstate ninety-five now and Hawk stared out through the tinted windows looking at the illuminated Miami skyline. Nearly twenty minutes passed, and they were on a long dark road with professional landscaping that was quickly turning into swampland. The outside was dark through the tinted window, and it seemed as if they were entering into another country. It was scary, something like a scene from a horror movie. The interior was dark inside the Hummer and the further they rode, the darker it got.

The Everglades was eerie for sure, it was sixty miles wide. The slowest moving river you'd ever see, and full with saw grass and deadly reptiles, including hungry alligators, crocodiles, and poisonous snakes. The river flowed southward to the end of the state. To the public in Miami and the other cities in south Florida, the Everglades was a national sightseeing park and tourist attraction. But to the underworld of Florida, it was also known as: No Witnesses.

The Hummer slowed down until it finally came to a complete stop. The rear passenger door came open where Carlos was sitting. He stepped down into the circle of four armed Colombians. With the specially made seats curving like the rear of a limousine, they made Hawk scoot around to the best of his ability. When he got to the door, one of the Colombians grabbed him around his feet and yanked him hard, causing him to bang his head against the chrome bar under the door. Blood began to leak instantly.

Hawk frowned as he felt the pain rushing through his body. He landed flat on his back and the Colombians burst into laughter.

Fly was helped down, then Smurf and the rest of them fell in the circle with the rest of the Colombians. Fly looked at Carlos. "How we gonna do it?"

Carlos spoke quickly in Spanish and then in a flash, one of the Colombians got underneath Hawk and flipped him up. He pulled him up by his neck and locked him in the inside of his elbow.

He growled in the deadliest tone of voice that Hawk had ever heard. "Apologize for your sins now, and save yourself from torture."

The Colombian was short and stocky with massive arms. When he didn't get a response from Hawk, he instantly applied pressure around his neck and started choking him. Locking his left arm around his right and pressing his hand against the back of Hawk's head.

He was just about to kill him when Fly yelled out, "Don't kill him." Fly stepped forward, his cane in his left hand. He moved directly in front of Hawk, looking him square in his eyes. He shifted his eyes to the Colombian. "Drop him." Fly said.

The Colombian dropped Hawk and he fell hard to the ground. Two blazing flashlights went to his face. His eyes had turned red, and he was panting hard, trying to catch his breath.

Fly moved up to him and sat the bottom of his cane on Hawk's chest. Staring down at him, he asked, "You must think this shit a game?"

Hawk was still lying in the damp grass, breathing heavily, not responding.

"I'm a respectful man, Hawk. And out of courtesy, I'll ask you to apologize again to save yourself from torture."

Hawk slowly turned his head upward and looked dead in Fly's eyes. He searched for the words and quickly blurted out, "I'm sorry."

Fly's eyes turned to slits. He reached inside his front pocket and came out with a small knife. He flipped out the blade, leaned down, cut his shirt down the middle and yanked it away from his body. Then he sliced is pants off and roughly ripped them away from his body. He backed away from him and looked at Smurf questioningly.

Cole Hart

"Whatever you wanna do," Smurf said.

"Put him where they can get to him. I want him to be alive."

"Alive?" One of the Colombians asked.

Fly eyes shifted to him, he nodded his head and repeated, "Alive."

Twenty minutes later, Hawk was stripped naked, tied, and bound. They'd put tiny cuts across his body and sat him down at the end of the dock. Hawk's feet were hanging over and his blood was dripping into the dark water. Fly stood back, a flashlight in his hand. Smurf stood next to him with a mini camcorder, filming the action.

When Hawk's body was snatched into the water, he hit with a big splash. The majority of the Colombians were closer to the edge, one of them holding the other end of the rope. Fly and Smurf walked forward.

Almost six high beam flashlights were aiming down into the muddy water where Hawk was being eaten alive by the alligators. They were spinning him around and ripping him apart. The water was turning darker by the second. The rope was snatched from the Colombian, and the splashing in the water grew louder. Hawk's head came to the top of the water and his eyes were frozen in terror. Then he went under again, and so did the gators.

After ten minutes, they stood in silence and listened to the feast until the water became still and calm. Smurf turned off the camera.

Without a word, they turned and headed back towards the Hummer.

Chapter 28

In Chia, Colombia, a bunker was something underground, like a small safe spot. However, the bunker that the Colombians had underground was more like an eight bedroom mansion. It was twenty feet below ground, with a main building and an east and west wing. The frames were built out of strong, solid steel beams and the walls were made from steel sheets on the outside. The luxurious interior was something out of the ordinary for a bunker underground.

The entire east wing belonged to Pepé, Falisa, and Amil. The master bedroom on the east wing was a huge, wide, spacious room with thick carpet. A super king sized bed was built into the floor with maple burl wood. A whirlwind Jacuzzi was built down inside the floor with gold faucets and knobs. Candles were lined around it, lit and giving off a vanilla scent. Inside the Jacuzzi, Amil was sitting in the hot water in a two-piece bikini, sipping on a virgin daiquiri from a straw and listening to Mary J. Blige from the hidden speakers built inside the wall. She was rolling her head and neck, and snapping her fingers in a seductive manner.

Her eyes were closed and she was swaying her glass in the air, when there was a knock at her door. She yelled, "Just a minute."

Amil sat her glass on the lip of the Jacuzzi and pushed herself up out of the water. Amil's body was curvy, her stomach was flat, and her legs were thick like a gymnast. She stepped out of the water, pulled her bikini bottoms from the crease of her ass, and walked towards the door. She unlocked it and pulled it open slightly.

Falisa was there. Her mother's face was glowing with energy and pure beauty. She had a towel around her head, and her body was wrapped in a silk robe.

Falisa pushed the door closed with her butt and her and Amil went to her bed and sat down next to each other. Amil had a folded towel on her bed. She grabbed it and wrapped it around her shoulders.

Her eyes went to Falisa, sensing that something was wrong. It wasn't showing on her face, so she asked her. "Is everything alright, Mother?"

Falisa fell backwards on the bed, her eyes staring towards the ceiling. Then she said, "You and Fly have a secret that you haven't shared with me, and I'm wondering why."

Amil got quiet, her eyes dancing all over Falisa in question. *She knows.* Amil said to herself. *Or does she? Has Fly told her? Are they testing my loyalty?* The conflicting thoughts raced through Amil's head. "Fly told me that Pepé chopped his leg off for no reason, and he and Smurf were held here in prison until you came here and gave yourself up in exchange for them."

"And you manipulated us to come over here so you could actually see everything for yourself. You're really here to kill Pepé, correct?" Falisa turned over on her side, her right elbow on the bed and her hand propped up her head. Her face is expressionless, staring directly at her daughter.

Amil didn't respond. Her eyes told the truth.

Falisa whispered, "I understand your feelings, baby." She reached and grabbed her hand, pulled it up to her mouth and kissed the back of it. "But what you are about to do will get our whole family wiped off the map. The Colombians are stronger than we are. We don't have a chance in hell."

Another long pause. Quiet sat between them. Then Amil asked, "So what happened to you when you turned yourself in to Pepé and his brothers?"

Falisa froze briefly, fearing the day that this question would come. She took a deep breath and felt butterflies in her stomach. Still holding on to Amil's hand, her eyes turned away from her. Falisa was nearly in tears just thinking about it.

Amil placed her hand under her mother's chin, laid down next to her, and stared her dead in her eyes, waiting for Falisa to respond.

A tear fell from her eye and Amil wiped it away with the back of her hand, feeling the pain from her mother. Falisa's bottom lip began trembling uncontrollably and she finally blurted out in a low whisper, "I was a sex slave." Falisa finally said and broke down in tears.

Amil reached over and hugged her tightly. She whispered in her ear. "Shhh, don't cry, mother. I'm eighteen now, and my final decision is that each of them should die."

"It's not easy like that, Amil. They're much stronger and fiercer. Our team is strong because of them. I married Pepé to get back to the United States and to make sure our family is wealthy."

"On my word, let me take my chance here. I won't jeopardize our family. I just need your approval."

"I can't co-sign that, Amil, it's too risky."

Amil's eyes got tight, no flinching her lashes or anything. She pulled her mother close and hugged her tight as if she was the daughter. "I understand, mother, truly I do. But what you don't understand is that I've already laid out the blueprint..."

A light knock came from the door and Pepé pushed it open. He walked in, holding a phone with a smile on his face. His white linen suit made him glow underneath the low ceiling light. Amil looked over at him and Falisa sat up, her moist eyes dried instantly because she didn't want Pepé to suspect anything. She stood up, recognizing the excitement in his eyes.

"Si, it's over. No problem." he said and opened his arms. Falisa fell straight into them and laid her head flat on his chest.

Amil got up from the bed and pretended to be happy go lucky about the small cartel war being over. She hugged the circle of Pepé and her mother. "That's the best news," Amil said cheerfully. "So when can we get out from down here? I really need some fresh air."

"Maybe two more days down here, until they get things up there cleaned up."

That's all Amil needed to hear. Two more days down there would be just enough time for her to do what she needed to do. She released Pepé and her mother at the same time. "I'm going to shower," she said while walking towards the marble shower with clear see through glass doors.

Pepé kissed Falisa on her lips and finally looked her in her eyes. He saw that she was bothered about something. "What's wrong?"

She quickly turned on yet another smile, revealing her even white teeth. She grabbed his face and held it, then kissed him passionately.

"You had me worried," she mumbled.

Across the room, Amil turned on the water in the shower. She came out, still dressed. "Well, maybe we could have dinner tonight. A big dinner for all of us."

Pepé and Falisa both turned toward her. "Sounds like a good idea." Pepé said.

Amil smiled, and then she pulled the outer curtain so she could take a quiet and peaceful shower.

Chapter 29

The Cartel family joined for dinner in a huge square room with low ceilings and twin chandeliers that gave off soft lighting. Underneath it was a full circle round table made out of white marble that was covered with a cocaine white lace cloth. Eight seats were occupied around the table. Pepé and Falisa sat next to each other. He was in shirt and pants, both pieces made of powder blue cool silk. Falisa wore a strapless dress in the same color. The light touches of makeup that she wore only enhanced her beautiful face.

Amil sat next to her mother. She was young and sexy this evening, wearing a full dress with a zipper down her back. Her hair was jet black and permed, hanging past her shoulders. Ten carats of high-grade expensive diamonds sparkled from each of her earlobes. Just she alone had brought light and excitement to the room.

Next to her was Cortez, Pepé's younger brother next to him. Then Carlos was beside him, the youngest of the three. The remaining seats were filled with their personal bodyguards. Everyone was strapped except Falisa and Amil. There were several bottles of Don Julio Tequila spread around the table. There were four bottles of The Macallan 1939, along with ice buckets of champagne and wooden boxes of Bolivar Cigars. Bowls of fresh fruit, platters of white rice and Spanish rice were on the table, as well as Pepé's personal dish of Mediterranean octopus and Key West pink shrimp. Cold bottles of water, three types of fish, and well-done steaks completed the meal. For the next hour, they ate, talked amongst themselves and laughed.

Amil and Falisa talked to each other, but Amil kept her ears in tune to the brothers' conversation. They spoke about cocaine numbers in Spanish and millions of dollars. Amil heard something about some rebellious women being locked up, and that they would be executed as soon as they came from out of the underground mansion. Amil looked around the table, glancing into everyone's eyes with a smile. She made most of the men uncomfortable.

She looked at Cortez, her supposed to be uncle that was seated next to her. "Uncle Cortez," she said softly, in a melodic tone.

Cortez looked at her, staring at her youthful beauty and tight flawless skin. "Yes, Amil?" His huge hand was laced around a glass and his eyes were getting low.

"If possible, when this is all over, will you show me the Coco fields?"

Cortez took it in quickly, but before he answered, his eyes cut over to Pepé in hopes that he would answer that question. Pepé looked at him, then stuffed two pink shrimp in his mouth and chewed. When he didn't respond, Cortez's eyes went to Falisa, but she wasn't even looking in his direction.

That left him speechless. His eyes went to Amil and he said, "Maybe."

"Maybe?" she asked in a cheerful voice. She held her hand up, her wrist bent in a feminine manner, waving her manicured nails. "Honestly, you won't hurt my feelings if you say no."

Cortez was experiencing conflicting emotions.

Amil looked at Pepé. She noticed that he was intoxicated and his eyes were low as well. She struck a conversation about the hippos and talked about things that caught their attention. Everyone joined in with the conversation, and while they talked, she allowed her left hand to slip underneath the table and touch Cortez's right knee.

Cortez became instantly alert. He wasn't expecting that. His eyes widened and he tried to laugh it off. When he felt her hand inching up his inner thigh, his heart began thumping harder inside his chest. But he didn't stop her. The Tequila had his head swimming. When he felt her hand grasp his penis, he reached into the center of the table where the expensive Bolivar cigars were sitting in a neat row. He got one and found himself shaking nervously.

When he sat back down, he felt Amil's hand between his legs again. He fired up his cigar right there, knowing he was violating their family rules by smoking at the table. He was nervous about Pepé, because if he knew what was going on, it would separate their loyalty. But he still didn't move Amil hand. He was hard and thick. She massaged him slowly while still talking to her mother.

The Throne 3

Cortez stood up quickly, pushing his chair back. The cigar was clenched between his teeth. Everyone looked at him. He placed his hand on his stomach as if it was hurting. "Excuse me." he said and exited the room. Everyone's head turned, watching him leave.

After Cortez left the room, everyone went back to talking and enjoying themselves, eating, drinking. Five minutes turned into fifteen and Cortez hadn't come back yet. Amil grabbed a glass of red wine, fumbled it by accident and wasted some on the bottom of her dress. Now all eyes were on her.

Falisa gave her a napkin and she wiped her dress, pretending to be embarrassed. "Excuse me." she said politely and exited the room as well.

When she got in the long corridor, it was quiet and lonely. Her heels clicked against the floor as she moved swiftly. When she got to the bathroom door, Cortez was coming out. She blocked him at the threshold, pushed him back inside, and locked the door behind them.

"No... we can't do this, Amil," he said in his broken English. He held his cigar pressed between his thumb and index finger.

Amil got up close to him, pressing her breasts hard against his chest. The smoke circulated around them. "Why? I'm not pretty enough? I don't turn you on, Cortez?" She went for his pants, tugging at the buttons and then pulled down his zipper. She took him out, staring down at it. This was her first time coming this close to a man. She massaged him with both hands. "It's so big," she whispered, staring straight into his eyes. "I'm still a virgin," she added for security.

Cortez's eyes widened when he heard the word virgin and his dick grew harder. Cortez sat his cigar down on the back of the toilet and lifted Amil up on the marble countertop. He got between her legs, pulled her lace panties to the side, and buried his face. He sucked and licked her like a mad man. Amil kicked her left leg up and ran her fingers through Cortez's hair while her eyes rolled to the back of her head. He made her cum in five minutes and sucked up all her juices.

"I want you to fuck me." Amil said in a begging tone.

Cortez stood up, turned on the water and began washing his face and rinsing out his mouth. He looked over at Amil; she was touching herself with her middle finger.

"You must keep this a secret, Amil," he said nervously.

"And if I don't?" She reached for him, clutched a fist full of his shirt and pulled him to her. "Don't tease me, Cortez. You've committed yourself now." She put her arms around his neck and leaned into him. "I promise on my life, it's our secret."

Cortez listened closely to her soft words, and then he kissed her on her lips.

Chapter 30

Smurf didn't have a mansion, but it was definitely a nice five-bedroom estate nestled on five acres of land in the outskirts of Atlanta, with an additional two-bedroom guesthouse out back. Inside the estate, Smurf, Fly and Pig Man were all sitting around lounging in Smurf's den. Iris and January were out shopping at Phipps for bridesmaid's gowns and other accessories for Smurf's wedding, which was coming up very soon. Fly would be the best man without a doubt, because Smurf wouldn't have it any other way. Smurf had his lounge room laid out comfortably. The walls were made of dark mahogany wood paneling and the overstuffed leather furniture was comfortable.

On the eighty-inch screen, they watched basketball highlights on ESPN. The left wall boasted a wet bar made of high gloss wood with glass shelves and a mirror behind the liquor bottles and glasses.

Pig Man sat back on the sofa, folded his arms across his chest, and looked at Fly, a faint smile on his lips. "What happened in Canada?" he asked.

Fly and Smurf were flipping through a wedding magazine, examining some of the best tuxedos that money could buy. Fly looked up at him, his eyes dancing in question. "What happened like what?"

"Wit' dat' nigga, Six. I wanna know the look on that nigga face when he found out you was you."

Fly's mind was totally on something else. He was hoping Amil and Falisa could make the wedding. But the way it was looking, that wasn't going to happen. Now Pig Man asking the normal crazy questions he always did, was throwing him off. "He was surprised." Fly said flatly.

Pig Man turned his head sideways, looking at Fly and trying to make him laugh. When he didn't, Pig Man shrugged and said, "Can't be serious all the time, youngsta." He straightened his head up and kept his arms folded.

"He turned gray almost. Especially when he found out we wasn't no damn Jehovah witness—" Fly began.

Pig Man cut him off. "Yawl use the Jehovah witness blueprint?" he asked, surprised.

"And it's official. Iris knows the bible inside out. She got right in with the grandmother off the top."

"Where Falisa be coming up with her blueprints?"

"Good question," Smurf said, then he added, "but Amil is the one."

The Throne 3

"Amil is good." Fly agreed with Smurf, then he looked back down at the magazine, flipped a couple more pages, and looked back up at Pig Man. "What it's looking like on Papa Bear?"

Pig Man smiled, his mouth dancing with sparkling diamonds. "He winning as of now. The attorney is arranging a three-year guilty plea. He confessed to fighting dogs and roosters. The feds don't care as long as they get a damn conviction. He should be at the federal halfway house in less than a year."

"That sounds real good." Fly said, his eyes scanning the room. "Man, I wish everybody could be here for the wedding. Papa Bear need to be here. Falisa and Amil need to be here. Damn."

He looked at Smurf who lifted his eyes from the magazine. "We can postpone the whole wedding if we need to," Smurf said nonchalantly.

Fly looked at Pig Man. He was the oldest of the three of them and he wanted to hear his opinion.

Pig Man looked from Fly to Smurf, his eyes darting between them. Quiet had settled in. Then Pig Man said, "Everybody would be upset if you postpone your wedding." He stood up, a faint smile covered his face and he began rubbing his hands together anxiously. Pig Man walked over to the bar, grabbed a bottle Dom Perignon, three long stemmed champagne glasses, and lined them up.

"We gon' drank to our success, and our nigga Smurf about to tie the knot." He popped the bottle. It bubbled up and ran over the side. He filled the three glasses. He carried one to Fly and one to

Smurf, and then held up his own glass. The three of them toasted and clinked their glasses together. "To the Throne." Pig Man said.

"To the Throne." Smurf said and looked at Fly.

"To the Throne." Fly repeated.

They all turned up their glasses and sipped.

Then Pig Man added, "I still say you should have a small private bachelor party. Just us and a couple bitches from the club."

"Gotta pass on that one, brah." Smurf said. He stood up and sipped the champagne again. He was in gray Jordan shorts and a wife beater. He faced Pig Man and said in a low casual tone of voice. "I'm just trying to do something simple."

"Ahh." Pig Man gave a light laugh. "I hear that, but brah when you playing wit' millions and white keys like we do, our simple shit ain't simple by far."

Fly nodded his head with a co-sign of Pig Man's statement and they all laughed for a moment. Then Smurf said, "Fuck it then. All white every thang. White horses, white carriage, white limos, white drivers." Smurf paused, turned up his glass and killed the remainder of his Dom.

"I feel that. I'ma wear the cocaine white tux, white diamonds."

"Man, yawl niggas done went white crazy."

Smurf walked over to the bar and poured another glass of champagne. He was lost in thought for a brief moment as he stared at the bubbles floating and rising inside the glass. He finally turned around and faced Pig Man and Fly. "It's been a change of plans. I'll have to push our date back on the strength of Falisa, Papa and Amil."

"Man, January gon' go ham." Pig Man said, laughing. Then the phone rang.

Outside, in front of the estate, January was behind the wheel of a black Mercedes Benz station wagon. Iris was on the passenger side, staring out the window and taking in the beautiful scenery. Their front lawn was green and manicured, and the sky was a crisp blue. They were listening to soft Jazz, which really relaxed them both. January slowed down as she got to the mouth of her ·driveway. When she turned up in her driveway, she noticed an ambulance was behind her with lights blazing and no sirens. She pulled the station wagon behind the all black Yukon that Pig Man was driving.

When she killed the engine, the front door opened and Smurf appeared with a cordless phone pressed against the side of his face. He surveyed the scene with a confused look.

January stepped out of the driver seat. She was in a sundress and heels, with a chiffon scarf tied around her neck. Iris stepped out, walked around to the rear of the station wagon, but before she could open it, Fly and Pig Man came out the door. They were all looking confused.

Pig Man went to the bottom of the stairs, walked to the rear of the station wagon, and opened the door just as the ambulance was backing into their driveway. Smurf was still on the phone with the

911 operator. "Yes ma'am, I understand that. An ambulance just pulled up in my driveway, but I can assure you that no one called them from this number or address." He hung up and looked over at Fly and Pig Man while walking toward January. "They got a mix up or something."

Just as he said that, the rear doors of the ambulance burst open from the inside and four men in black Nomax flight suits, full body armor, ski masks and armed with pistol grip Ithaca shotguns appeared. They spread out in a line and took aim.

One of the masked men yelled out angrily, "Brooklyn nigga." He squeezed the trigger and the first person that got hit was Iris.

Then the games began, the guns came out and they returned fire. Pig Man removed a fully automatic handgun from the waistline of his pants, his eye stretching wide. He saw Iris laying on the asphalt at the rear of the station wagon. She was bleeding and holding her stomach. When he let the first round go, it sounded like the drum line from a marching band. He was running forward, Fly was unarmed and the only thing he could do was try to get to Iris.

Smurf returned fire with a Glock .40, but the twelve gauge shells were coming hard and fast. When he felt the searing pain hit him, the impact knocked him off his feet. Glass was falling from the automobile windows. Fly managed to get to Iris and pull her to the rear of the Yukon, holding her stomach, her face in pain. Shots were ringing out and sounding closer and closer.

Fly thought about the AKs that were in the rear of the Yukon. He went to the rear passenger door and opened it, but it was too

Cole Hart

late. The four masked men were back inside the ambulance and they were still opening fire. Iris was hit, as was Pig Man and Smurf. Fly hadn't seen January. He knelt down, clutching the AK 47. He looked underneath the Benz station wagon and saw January laying in a puddle of her own blood.

All he could say was, "Damn! Hawk retaliated. Son of a bitch."

Chapter 31

A few days later, Pepé and Falisa gave permission for Cortez to take Amil to see one of the huge industrial-sized fields of coca where the stalks grew and where they had a huge cocaine production lab that resembled a military barrack. Cortez knew he could break Amil if he took her through jungles to another part of Colombia in a small community called La Balsa. La Balsa was small and compact, housing the poor Afro-Colombians in homes that were made from wood planks and tin roofs. They were the people that worked and processed the cocaine, day in and day out to make ends meet for their families.

Just getting there was a job in itself. They hiked through the jungle on foot, Amil, Cortez, and several men from their organization. Each person was outfitted in military issued fatigue uniforms and boots. Then they had to cross a creepy river by boat, just to deploy and hike a narrow trail for another two hours. Soaked in sweat, her shirt clinging to her skin and covered with bumps from insect bites on her neck and arms, Amil was unstoppable. She wore her hair pinned up in a neat ball and smothered down by a fatigue cap that was pulled down over her eyes.

Cole Hart

The Throne 3

When they finally entered the lab, the ether smell was horrible. There were black women that looked just like her, dressed in rag clothes and wearing hospital masks over their nose and mouths. They were churning the coca leaves into paste in huge pots. She looked from side to side. Some women were shirtless, walking around, pouring sweat, with their breasts exposed, carrying huge stalks of coca on their shoulders. The majority of the men were doing the heavy labor, pushing wheelbarrows of cocaine and loading it with shovels inside of steel drums.

Amil walked through quietly, not asking one question as she took in the scenery and realized that America wasn't the only place where Africans were slaves. She walked, she studied, she took mental notes, and then she stopped. She removed her cap and wiped the sweat from her face with the back of her hand.

She looked at Cortez. "It's so hot in here," she said.

Cortez's eyes were on her. "You ready to leave now?" he asked her.

She shook her head. "Where do you keep the prisoners?"

Cortez's eyes narrowed a little. He studied her, wanting to ask her why she wanted to see the prisoners. He decided against it and walked ahead of her. He went toward the rear of the building where a wide spacious opening was. Amil followed him to a wide concrete slab where yellow forklifts were organizing wood crates of cocaine that was ready to be shipped.

Amil was carefully taking it all in. She already knew the cocaine numbers the prices here and the prices in America. Falisa

Cole Hart

166

had a lot of say so, but here, her eyes were bigger and she wanted more for the family. When she finally focused her eyes on Cortez, he jumped from the concrete slab three feet to the ground. He was standing below motioning his arm for Amil to come on down.

Without hesitation, she jumped three feet down, landed safely onto the soft dirt, and playfully went into Cortez's arms. She smiled, and then pulled away, realizing that their soldiers were behind them and they needed to keep their relationship under the radar. They turned around and hiked deeper into the jungles. Cortez let four of his men lead the way with their weapons drawn. After about a quarter of a mile, there was an opening. To their left was a building made of cinder blocks, steel doors and a tin roof. The cell doors had numbers ranging from one to fifty on the front facing side, and fifty-one to one hundred on the backside.

Another amazed look spread across Amil's face. She walked straight over to the first steel door. She removed a lock, only sliding it backwards and then pulled open the small door. She looked through a small glass that was six by nine in size, and filthy. She squinted and couldn't see anything.

Out of nowhere, an unusually ugly face appeared. Amil jumped back and bumped into Cortez. He put his hands on the small of her back while she placed her hand on her chest and smiled. "He scared me."

"He can't hurt you." Cortez said in her ear. His thick, Spanish accent sounded good to her. She looked back at him for a brief moment, giving him a smile and a seductive look. Then she went back to the window and looked in. The prisoner had quickly cleaned the window from the inside. Amil got a better look at him;

he was dark skinned, with marble-green eyes and enough hair on his face and head to make him look like an animal. He stared straight into her eyes.

Amil saw too much fear in him for some reason, and then she spoke to him in Spanish. "Hello."

He responded back to her with a simple "Hello." His words came like a growl. No other words were exchanged.

She closed the small window door and put the latch back on. She went to door two, opened the small door and looked through the window. There was a small frame laying in a cot at the back of the small cell, underneath a blanket. Amil tapped on the glass and the cover began moving. A head appeared. It was a light-skinned woman who looked Chinese. She moved the covers from her body. She was naked. Her body was fragile, her chest was flat, and her ribcage was visible. The closer she got to the door, the more Amil's stomach turned.

The woman came to the window and looked at Amil. Amil stared back. She saw strength in the fragile woman, no fear, whatsoever. In Spanish, she asked Amil, "Who are you?"

Before Amil could respond, Cortez came up behind her and closed the flap to the window. Amil turned around and stared at him. Questions burned in her eyes. Cortez shook his head slowly, and in a whispering tone, he said, "She no good to us. Very dangerous."

"What did she do?" Amil asked. She removed her cap again and wiped the pouring sweat.

The girl began beating on the window from the inside. Cortez's eyes went to the door, and then he grabbed Amil's hand and pulled her away from the rest of his Cartel, and out of earshot of the prisoners.

"These people are very dangerous, Amil. She's a member of a rival Cartel and she'll be executed very soon. Just like everyone else here."

Amil nodded her head one time in agreement and she removed her hand from his. "I understand," she said. But in her mind, her understanding was zero. She was a tough cookie and she wanted it her way. She walked to the third door alone, while Cortez and his men stayed back and watched her. The Colombians fired up cigarettes and cigars while they watched Amil go down the row, door to door, looking in on all of them, speaking and holding conversations at every other door.

Cortez stood to the side, away from his men all except his main lieutenant, a huge Colombian with a large head and wide shoulders. He watched Amil intently, and asked Cortez, "What's her plan?"

Cortez pulled his cigar, watched Amil's shapely body from the back and just shook his head while the smoke curled up around his face. "I don't know," he said.

But he soon would.

Chapter 32

At the all-white mansion in Chia, Falisa was on the phone with Fly. Standing in the middle of the living room floor in a white sundress, she was worried, but Fly assured her that everything was all right. In her heart, she knew it wasn't. He'd told her that Pig Man was dead, and so was January. Smurf was on life support and Iris lost the baby. Fly sounded weak to her. She knew her son, and he wasn't all right. There were funeral arrangements that had to be made and Fly couldn't do it all by himself.

"I'll be in Atlanta tomorrow," she said into the phone. Before he could respond, she hung up.

She turned, looked at Pepé, who was sitting in a double stuffed leather chair looking up at her. He stood, recognizing the saddened look in her eyes. When the tears came, he wrapped his arms around her and held her close. She cried on his shoulder, and he comforted her the best he could.

She snapped back away from him. "We got to go, Pepé," she said.

Pepé looked at her, his thick eyebrows furrowed. "We still can't leave yet, Falisa."

"What?" She frowned. Her voice rose to another level, and she shot Pepé the deadliest look that she could.

Pepé pulled her into his arms and she felt his strength. Falisa was desperately trying to pry away, tears rushing from her eyes. "Let me go to my son, damnit." She reached up and clawed his face with her nails.

Pepé was stunned. The cut from her nails felt like razors. Out of anger, he threw her hard to the floor, took two steps forward and stood over her. His eyes turned to slits, looking like a cobra that was about to strike.

Both of the French doors unexpectedly flew open. Pepé looked up, knowing he would see his brother Carlos or either Cortez coming in. No one else had the key or the access code, but he was wrong, and not by far. When he saw his own lieutenant enter, he almost smiled until he saw Amil fall through the door behind him with a compact forty-five automatic gripped tightly in her hand.

He was confused; especially when he saw the black Colombians enter through the door. The four females and four males that they had in lock up in La Balsa were all heavily armed and dangerous. Everybody was in all black, except for Amil. She was in fatigues and boots.

The lieutenant raised his side arm and aimed it at Pepé. "Your brother raped your daughter," he said in his thick Spanish accent. "She said she told you about it and you didn't believe her."

Pepé mustered a grin. His eyes turned evil and stared dead into his. "And you believed that, you fucking, traitor? Where the fuck are my brothers?"

Amil stepped forward. She raised the gun to his eye level, and then she looked down at her mother, not knowing why she was laying on the floor crying. That made her even angrier. Her lips tightened, and then she tightened her grip around the gun. Her finger was hard on the trigger. The rest of the black Colombians spread out and moved through the mansion like navy seals.

"It's a new cartel, Pepé. And you're not a part of it." She pulled the trigger. The forty-five roared, and a slug slammed directly into the center of Pepé's forehead. When he fell, he landed next to Falisa with his eyes wide open.

She turned and looked at him, staring through his eyes and into his soul. She reached and flipped his eyelids closed. The lieutenant extended his hand. She grabbed it and he pulled her up to her feet. A spray of blood was splashed across her white dress. Amil hugged her mother with her left arm and held the gun tightly in her right.

"All of them are dead, Pepé was the last one."

"That's good, but we must go to the states now. The family was ambushed in Atlanta. Pig Man and January are dead. Smurf is on life support."

Amil gasped. Her hand flew to her mouth. "What about Fly and Iris?"

"Fly wasn't hurt, but Iris was hit."

Cole Hart   172

Amil took a deep breath. She was devastated by Falisa's words, and out of anger, she dropped her aim on the forty-five, locked it in on Pepé's motionless face, and squeezed the trigger, slamming three more slugs into his face. The bullets tore holes in his face the size of piranhas.

She looked at Falisa, fighting back her tears. "You got to go without me, Mother."

"It's not an option, Amil. I can't leave you here alone. Are you crazy?"

Amil smiled, kissed her cheek again, and then she turned to the huge lieutenant. His name was Juan. "Make sure my mother gets to the jet safely, and then to the states."

Falisa grabbed Amil around her wrist and yanked her closer to her. "What the fuck are you doing, Amil?" she growled in a low tone.

She whispered in her mother's ear. "Securing your position on the Throne, now let me do me, baby. It's a new pink print I got in the making." She gave Falisa a quick peck on her lips. "I'm a big girl, and I learned from the best."

Falisa nodded, turned away from Amil and looked up at Juan. Side by side, they walked through the double French doors.

Amil watched them fade away from her eyesight.

———

Cole Hart

The Throne 3

Falisa was on her feet now, standing next to her chair and pouring a glass of champagne in a long stem glass, she poured it until the glass began running over and spilling onto the table. Out of her peripheral vision, she saw the nurse watching her, fascinated.

In a slow saddened voice, she said, "Please don't tell me that's the ending."

Falisa drank her glass down some, and then she walked the measured ten feet to the other end of the table where her nurse sat. Falisa poured her champagne. The nurse grabbed her glass and Falisa held her glass up. Their glasses clinked together, and it sounded like Jingle Bells in the room.

"To greatness," Falisa said.

"To greatness." The nurse repeated confidently. She sipped lightly, feeling a slight dizziness in her head. "So what happened with Amil?"

Falisa stood over her, looking down at her. "She vanished," she said slowly and slightly cold.

"What do you mean, vanished?"

Falisa walked back to her end of the table, carrying her glass in one hand and the bottle in the other. She sat them both down, then she removed her tuxedo jacket from the back of the chair and draped it across her shoulders. She turned her focus back on the nurse. "Did I say I was finished?" Falisa checked her watch. Time was winding down. "You know I had to save the best part for last."

"So this is it, no cliffhangers?" The nurse asked. She grimaced as the nasty acid vomit taste came from her stomach and up into her throat.

"No more cliffhangers, darling." she said. "But guess what the best part of the story is?" Falisa said brightly.

The nurse smiled brightly and tried to guess. For the next five minutes, she threw out guesses and Falisa kept telling her, "One more guess."

"I can't guess it. Just tell me, please." The nurse was begging. She wanted the rest of the story as if her life depended on it.

Pain flashed across the nurse's face. Falisa turned and walked back, taking long slow strides toward her nurse, maintaining eye contact. Falisa was locked in on her, and the closer she got, the more emotion she felt. Falisa stopped next to her. The nurse stared up at her. The room was quiet. Unspoken emotions seemed to battle in the stillness.

Finally, Falisa's words came from her mouth, low and calm, but they were filled with lava. "The best of the best is always saved for last. And that is, I just wanted to let you know that I'm quite aware that you're an undercover federal agent." Falisa didn't want to look her in her eyes any longer.

"That's not true."

Falisa turned on her heels again, heading back towards her end of the table, sipping her champagne as she went. When Falisa turned and looked at her nurse, she was already beginning to go into convulsions. Her eyes were stretched wide, and her throat felt like someone was burning her with a blowtorch.

"Heeelpp." The nurse's words barely escaped her mouth.

"Did you eat the syrup?" Falisa asked calmly.

The nurse's eyes widened even further, then she began pulling at her neck and nodding her head at the same time.

"I trusted you with my life. I shared my world with you. That's why I stressed to you the importance of slippers counting. I slipped and let you in. You slipped and ate the poison." When Falisa laughed, she turned toward the door and checked her watch. She knew she only had a few minutes before the place would be swarmed with federal agents. She looked back at the nurse, who was now foaming at the mouth and shaking uncontrollably.

Falisa blew her one kiss and whispered. "Kiss of death."

Outside in the parking lot, the Boca Raton, Florida skies were cloudy and gray. A light misty rain fell to the asphalt where the beige carpet cleaner van was parked. Inside the van, the two federal agents that had come and spoken with Falisa before were listening and recording the whole conversation. They both heard Falisa make the undercover agent. They snatched their earpieces from their ears, slid their vests on top of their shirts, and then got their weapons ready and threw on their blue DEA windbreakers.

The first agent chambered his weapon and opened the door. The agent in the rear was already calling for back up. They knew she couldn't get away. When they hopped down from the rear of the van, they ran as fast as they could towards the front entrance of the sanatorium.

No sooner than they entered, Falisa came from the side, walking casually and nervously, squinting her eyes against the drizzling rain. She walked through a small flowerbed, and then she heard a helicopter in the distance. She noticed the street, where a long funeral was coming up from her left. She made it to the street, just as the black hearse and the first limousine were passing. All the cars were majority Lincolns and Navigators, and every vehicle had their headlights on and a funeral sticker in the window.

She walked, legs chopping like scissors. When the third limousine got to her, the rear door opened. Falisa's heart rumbled inside her chest. The limo hadn't completely stopped, so she sped up and nearly dived inside. Papa Bear reached and pulled the door closed, after she got in.

She went straight into his arms and held on to him. "I'm nervous," she whispered.

Papa Bear held Falisa in his arms. He smelled her neck, drew back a little, and they looked in each other's eyes. Slowly, their lips met. That relaxed her. She rubbed her right hand down the side of his face and he rubbed her face with his left.

"All you do is relax. Let me do the worrying from here. You're in good hands." He slid over toward the other side of the limousine and looked out through the tinted window.

The Throne 3

The hearse came to a stop. There was a roadblock, and he knew it was the feds. He craned his neck and looked up. There were two helicopters, one flying above the line of cars. On the floor, Papa Bear had a retractable stock AK, fully automatic with a hundred round drum underneath a black beach towel. He flipped over the small cabinet and pulled out a black veil that was attached to an elderly woman's hat. Looking through the window, he saw that the feds had the hearse surrounded.

"Shit!" Papa Bear said. He looked at Falisa and handed her the hat and veil. "Put this on."

She pulled it down over her face. Papa Bear didn't recognize her. He motioned his hand for her to come to him, Falisa slid across the seat and he put his arm around her. "Now cry," Papa Bear whispered.

When Falisa thought about all that she had endured over the last few years, from the plane crash that had left her seriously injured, to the grueling recovery for the second time, the tears came easily. She thought about the isolation she felt from being locked away from her loved ones for two years, the stress of pretending to be an invalid, and finally the nervous joy of being reunited with Papa Bear. Sobs wracked her body as she embraced life and freedom.

Papa Bear rolled his window down. The streets were crawling with agents that were armed and in suits, others were in fatigues, but they were dead serious. When the agents finally got to their limousine, Falisa cried out as if she was in pain. She yelled and screamed, and Papa Bear even pretended that a tear fell from his eye. He was holding her head and whispering, "Shhh. It's gonna be alright."

A white federal agent looked inside, his badge hanging around his neck. He looked at Papa Bear, then to Falisa and then scanned the inside of his limousine. He felt the emotions and waved them on. Papa Bear pressed the button and the window went up. Falisa kept her head on his chest, but she was quiet.

"Told you I got you." he whispered, removed her veil, and then kissed her again.

Made in the USA
Lexington, KY
19 August 2015